To the amazing women of Delta Phi Epsilon Sorority, Delta Omega Chapter. An extra shout out to: Chris E., Jennifer S., Phyllis, Danette, Lisa T., Alisa, Darlane, Candice, Caroline, Jennifer M., Doreen, Denise, Lisa L., Andrea, Sheree, Jodi, Patti, Jane, Deb H., and Yamel
Thank you for your love, friendship, and constant support. You are the family I chose.
"Esse quam videri"

THE LAST BETRAYAL

BROTHERHOOD PROTECTORS WORLD

STACEY WILK

Twisted Page Press LLC

BROTHERHOOD PROTECTORS

ORIGINAL SERIES BY ELLE JAMES

CHAPTER 1

Eden King believed family came first. She also believed in getting the scoop. When the two mixed like whiskey and greasy beef nachos, her stomach fought back. She placed a hand on her middle to keep her dinner from making a reappearance. Johnny would not appreciate her vomiting on the table.

They sat tucked in a dark corner of Patrick's Steak House. The wood paneled walls, low ceilings, and dim lighting offered the best place for someone to share a secret. The backs of the wooden booths were high and blocked the view from the other patrons. Televisions were strategically placed around the open room. Their sounds of newscasters and sporting events drowned out the real conversations.

She had chosen this place to tell Johnny about the new information she'd discovered because for one, it was their favorite place to hang out, and two, he wouldn't make a scene in public. Johnny was known for making scenes.

She smoothed the napkin on her lap. "I have proof."

"Proof of what?" He came up out of his cheesy chips covered in jalapenos like a diver coming up for air.

All the King men resembled each other with their sandy brown hair and eyes the color of amber. They all possessed a strong jaw, long eyelashes, and the need for power. Except her father. He wanted family more than power, and that's what made him the black sheep of an influential family. Somehow, she and her cousin Johnny managed to be close even though his father, her uncle, craved power as if it were water.

She swallowed the knot in her throat to continue. "I can prove your father committed that crime."

He dropped his fork with a clang. "What are you talking about?"

"I am in possession of video evidence proving your father assaulted a woman while he was in college." She squared her shoulders. Uncle Thomas had sought a Supreme Court seat his entire career, and now all his dreams were about to end.

She would be the one to do it because even though family mattered most, the truth was just as important. Her job required her to report the news without bias. It didn't matter who was involved. Her uncle would not get away with raping a woman and then saying that woman lied about it. Not when Eden had the proof.

And if breaking this story finally gave her the credentials and notoriety she craved, so be it. She wanted – no, needed - to prove herself. She was more than just her family's name.

"You're lying."

"I'm afraid not. I'm sorry, Johnny. I needed you to know before I broke the story." Eden placed two twenties on the table. "I have to go." She grabbed her tote and her rain coat.

Her cousin gripped her wrist and leaned across the table. "You're going to drop a bomb like that and just run?" He whispered his words like the cobra Nag to Rikki-Tikki-Tavi. His hazel-eyed gaze darted side to side as if he were checking for big ears nearby. A flush crept up his neck.

"I wanted to warn you that I'm running with this story in twenty-four hours because you and I are close. If you have any loose ends to tie up, do it. I don't want you getting caught in the cross fire." She slid from the booth before he could say anything else.

His footsteps followed her out into the parking lot. The Montana spring night had a bite to it. The thick clouds promised more rain. She was ready for summer and ready to go home. She wanted to put her feet up, drink another shot of Jim Beam Honey, and come to terms with crushing the King family. Her father couldn't do it. He'd been a coward. Now she had to do what Samuel King could not accomplish before the Grim Reaper had come along and tapped his shoulder. Her father left her alone and at an ugly, dark cross-roads. If only he'd kept his mouth shut. She wouldn't know what Uncle Thomas had done and how to find the proof. Now that she knew, she had no choice.

"Eden, wait." Johnny gripped her arm and swung her around.

She teetered on her skinny heeled pumps. "Christ, Johnny. Let go." She yanked her arm away.

He threw his hands up. "Sorry. I have to tell my father."

"So tell him. I don't care. He's going to read about it anyway."

"What if your proof is wrong?" He ran a hand through his thick hair.

"It's not. I saw it." She had not seen it, but she'd view the tape before she handed in her story.

"If you do this, you'll drag me down too. I'm up for a promotion. Do you think the captain will give me a gold shield if my father has been convicted of a sexual assault?"

"You're not your father. What he did has nothing to do with you. You weren't even born when this happened." She paused. "Unless you have something to hide too."

She prayed he was clean, but knew the reality of a cop's life. Plenty of them took bribes or skimmed off the top of drug money about to be confiscated and destroyed. Who was going to miss a few thousand when a child needed braces? She had never asked Johnny. Ignorance was bliss when it came to her family.

"Of course I have nothing to hide. But we're family. He's my father. You'll ruin his life. Do you think it's what Uncle Samuel would have wanted?"

Her father didn't want his brother tried and convicted. That was why he hid the evidence all these years. But Uncle Thomas had done one too many things wrong on his way up the ladder, and her father had had one too many drinks. He'd spilled. Now she knew too.

"I have an obligation to report the truth no matter

who it affects. Not to mention, there's a woman who was hurt and needs closure. Your father had no right."

"It was thirty years ago. Why does it matter now? What if she was lying? Maybe she begged him to take her to bed. Did you think of that? She could have been coming onto him. He was a young guy. A girl told him yes. So he went with it."

Her blood turned to ice. "Who are you? Are you seriously going to stand there and tell me it was okay to rape a woman because she was drunk?" She wanted to put her hands around his neck and shake him.

"You don't know it was rape."

According to her father's admission, the tape only showed her uncle and the woman entering the room. "Even if the tape showed her interested in your father no still means no."

"Maybe she wanted it. Maybe she liked it rough. It's her word against his. He said the sex was consensual, and now you're going to produce some fucking old tape as proof? That doesn't prove anything. Why didn't she go to the hospital? Tell a friend? Why wait thirty years?"

"You're panicking. I understand that."

"What I'm fucking doing is trying to save my father. You can't go through with this. Please, I beg you." His voice shook.

Her heart ached for him. They were more like siblings than cousins. It had always been her and her father, but Uncle Thomas and Aunt Carol had included them in everything. She'd grown up with John. They went to the same schools, ran in similar circles, and had handed him tissues when his first girlfriend dumped him. She supported his decision to go into law enforcement instead of following his father's judicial path.

"I'm sorry. I don't have a choice." She dug her keys out of her tote and unlocked her car door.

"At least think it through." Tears filled his eyes.

"I've already thought about it. I can't allow a crime to go unpunished no matter who it is. I don't want to be related to man who could hurt a woman like that. He doesn't have the right to get away with rape."

"You're making a mistake."

"It's a mistake I can live with. I've got to go, John. I'll text you when the story breaks."

"Don't fucking bother. If you do this, we're through. You'll have no one and nothing. My mother will stop speaking to you too. Have you even thought about her in any of this?"

"Of course I have. I don't want to hurt her. I love her like a mother, but your father has no right to get away with this. He doesn't deserve a seat on the Supreme Court. What kind of man can carelessly hurt a woman? No, I'm sorry. This has to be done. Good night."

She didn't wait for him to respond again. She slid into the driver's seat and kicked over the car. Without a look back, she navigated the parking lot and headed for home.

She made a right at the traffic light. Bright headlights caught her eye in the rearview mirror. She shifted in her seat and turned up the music. At the next light, she turned left and so did the car behind her. Every street to her house would become less traveled. She yanked the steering wheel at the last second and sped down a side street. The car behind her kept going straight. Her chest loosened.

"I'm imagining things, is all. John had me worked up," she said to the dashboard.

She circled around to the road home. She'd pour a big glass of whiskey, put on her favorite sweats, and watch mindless television tonight. She needed to decompress because in twenty-four hours, her world would blow wide open. It was the exact punch her career needed. She'd finally make a real name for herself with this scoop. She wished it wasn't at the expense of her family, but her father should not have told her about the tape and where she could find it. He couldn't expect her to ignore that information, could he? His intentions no longer mattered. He was gone, and she was alone.

She turned down her street. The darkness was as thick as black velvet. The road had no street-lights or side-walks. The only light penetrating the black was from her front stoop and her neighbors' porch across the street. The other house on the street was closed up for the night. The small number of homes was the reason she purchased the tiny cottage. She didn't have time for friends or lovers. She'd sworn off serious relationships with men seven years ago, and she never really understood the dynamics of best friends. Somehow, she always disappointed the women in her life.

She pulled into the driveway and pushed out into the cold night air. At least the rain had stopped, but her front walk was covered in three inches of water from the last soak. Her new shoes were going to get ruined. She pulled them off and stuck them in her tote. All she wanted was to get inside.

She tip-toed through the water and wiggled the key in the lock. The front door opened with a shove from her shoulder.

The dark house sent shivers over her skin. She had forgotten to leave a light on before she left this morning, and the heater was set low to save money. She couldn't think about conserving energy or her bank account without thinking about Jax. *Not tonight.* She pushed the thought away and changed out of her work clothes and into her comfy sweats.

She poured a hefty glass of whiskey, ready to unshed the stress of the day. The flash of light outside her front window made her turn. No one came down her street unless they meant to. Tires crunched on her driveway. She grabbed her phone just to be safe.

The doorbell rang. She gathered her nerves and peered through the peep-hole. The tension drained from her shoulders, and she opened the door. "For Christ's sake, John, you scared the hell out of me showing up at this hour. Go home. There's nothing you can do to help your dad. He has to live with the consequences."

"Eden, I want that tape. Is it here?" John pushed past her into the house.

She wasn't going to tell him where she'd stashed the evidence. "It doesn't matter. I made a copy."

She had done no such thing. The tape was an old mini VHS tape and she hadn't had a chance to convert it. Her plan was to go to a small photo shop, have them convert it, and then watch it.

She'd fudged a little about the twenty-four hours. No one had this kind of evidence because no one had the inside track like she did. Even in forty-eight hours, she'd be ahead of her competition. That was why she could take tonight off before she had to hit the ground running, and she needed the rest. Losing her father had taken its toll on her. Arguing with John would ring her out like a dirty dish rag.

"Go home, John."

He ran a hand over his face and scratched at his day-old beard. Dark moons hung under his eyes and lines of exhaustion etched his face. "Yeah. Okay. You're right. I should back off and go home. It's just that it's my dad. He's my hero."

She hadn't meant to hurt him in all of this. "Come into the kitchen. I have some whiskey." Maybe their relationship could remain intact after this was all over.

A hard punch slammed into her back. Her arms splayed out in front of her. Her feet left the ground before her chin collided with the wide-planked wood floor.

John's hands gripped her ankles. He dragged her face down into the living room. She grasped for something to stop her from sliding, but her fingers slipped from the table leg. The doorway was out of reach. "Let go." She twisted, but he kept going.

He flipped her over onto her back and stared down at her. "Tell me where the tape is and this stops here." His eyes turned stone cold.

Ice formed in her belly, and her heart climbed into her throat. She tried to scramble into a sitting position, but slipped on the edge of the area rug. "John, please. Let's talk about this."

"Talking ended an hour ago." He yanked her up by the collar of her sweatshirt.

Her feet dangled in the air, but she held his empty stare. Her bladder almost released its contents down her leg.

"Where is it?" Spit formed at the corner of his mouth.

She batted his head with her arm. He tried to duck, but couldn't while he still held onto her. She swung again and he groaned. He dropped her like burning oil, and she landed on her tailbone. Sharp pain raced up her spine.

He grabbed her by the hair and yanked her head back. Her mouth fell open, and his fist collided with her face. Constellations formed before her eyes.

"Give me the damn tape."

"I don't have it here." And even if she did, she wouldn't tell him.

He hit her again. The edges of her vision turned black. She couldn't pass out. He'd kill her, and no one would convict Detective John King of murder.

"Get up." He loomed over her.

Her back was pressed against the couch, and her legs were under the coffee table. Her head spun, but she had to focus. She needed help, but from whom? Who would protect her from her cousin or uncle?

"I said to get up." Veins popped out on his neck.

She pulled her legs in, but he didn't wait for her to stand. He gripped her under the arm and wrenched her up. His fingers dug into her flesh. "Why are you doing this?"

"Because I will not allow you to hurt my father or me."

"What are you hiding?" There had to be more than just his need to protect his father's reputation. "Did you know about this?"

His vacant stare filled her bowels with water.

"The woman who accused my father of attacking her was nothing but trash. She tried to blackmail him by saying she'd retract her statement if he paid her, but he wouldn't be bought by some slut. He deserves that spot on the Court and your father was just a jealous, washed-up old man who had nothing and no one. My father is revered, a king just like our name."

"You're sick."

"Give me the tape." His hot breath blew her hair back.

"I don't have it here." She tilted her chin up.

He punched her in the gut and she doubled over. The wind was knocked from her lungs. She coughed and gagged. He kicked her in the side and she toppled like a rotted tree and hit her head on the coffee table. Her vision faltered. The black edges crept in closer. He lifted her up by her collar again and slapped her across the face over and over until her lip split open. He cocked back his arm and hauled off. His fist hit her below the eye. Her head snapped back. He spit on her.

"You have twenty-four hours to produce that tape. The only reason you're not dead right now is because we were close."

He tugged his shirt into place, turned on his heel, and closed the door behind him.

Tears spilled down her cheeks and blood ran over her chin. Every part of her body hurt. She fought to stay conscious. She needed to get out of there. Throw some clothes in a bag and high-tail it to New York where she'd hidden the tape. Sending the evidence half-way across the country seemed like a stupid idea at the time, but now she was glad she did.

She forced her arms to lift her to a sitting position and her shaking legs to stand. Her ribs protested, but she kept moving. She didn't have time to fix her cuts. There was only one place she could go.

She promised herself she'd stay away from him. She'd broken his heart and he probably still hated her with every right. She'd been selfish and cold when he needed her most. Now she needed him because no one else could keep her safe.

She'd kept tabs on him the past seven years. Knew where he lived. Knew what he did for a living. Knew him well enough to know he'd never turn her away if she showed up broken and bleeding. His heart was too big, no matter how bitchy she'd been to him. But she always loved him. She never stopped. She just couldn't give him what he wanted. She'd been afraid.

She managed to get on her sneakers and drag herself outside. John's vehicle was gone. The street was quiet. She took a few steps and vomited on the wet sidewalk. Her head spun more, but she had to get there.

She had to get to Jax.

CHAPTER 2

AJAX MONTERO CLOSED his suitcase and joined his friends. Tomorrow he'd leave for New York. Nothing would stop him from sitting in the front row of the parole hearing. He went every time the perp, the guy who ended his SWAT career, came before the board. That scum would never see the light of day if he could help it.

And he could.

He planned for a few extra days on this trip to act like a tourist in the big city. He was overdue for a vacation. As much as he loved Eagle Rock and the vast Montana sky, every once in a while, he enjoyed the lights and noise of the concrete jungle. He hoped the spring weather in New York would be kinder to his aching leg than the wet Montana weather. He rubbed the spot above his knee with his knuckles. No matter how much he worked out, that old bullet wound acted up during the rainy season. The smell of warm bread and grilled beef met him on the way to the kitchen.

"Jax, dinner is ready. What time is your flight?" Lincoln wiped his hands on the full-body apron hanging from his neck.

He bit into a sweet, red pepper. "You look like my mother in that thing."

"I think he's cute." Serra slapped Linc's butt and smiled up at him. Linc grimaced in return.

"You two need to get a room. I'm on the nine a.m. You sure I can't convince you to come along?"

Linc wrapped an arm around Serra's shoulders and pulled her close. "No, thanks. I hate all that traffic and people pushing and shoving each other. Plus, I don't want to leave this one."

Serra smiled up at Linc as if Jax wasn't even in the room. He shook his head. He had been in love like that once, but she cut his heart out of his chest with a dull knife and left him bleeding in his chair. He'd sworn off relationships after that.

"He's still over-protective since the whole Lazarus Crow thing. Even though Crow is tucked safely behind bars and isn't coming after me any longer."

"My woman can't be too careful." Linc plated the steaks.

"You're a Neanderthal, and I love that about you." She kissed Linc's cheek.

"Okay, you two are making my teeth hurt." He grabbed the plates and placed them on the table. "Linc, who's working with you while I'm away?"

"Hank let me bring Zane on to cover for you. He's thinking about joining the Brotherhood Protectors permanently. We'll see." Linc handed him a beer and Serra a glass of red wine. They took their places at the kitchen table.

"Isn't it great he and Zane are getting along?" Serra passed the mashed potatoes.

"About time." He tapped his beer with Linc's. Linc and his brother had drifted apart after their older brother died, but because Serra was in Linc's life again, he'd made an attempt to get closer to Zane.

"We can't all be like the Montero family. What are there, like twenty of you?" Linc said.

"Five, smart-ass. I'd like to see my brothers join the Brotherhood too. It's a family."

"Don't you have a sister? What about her?" Serra said.

"I don't want her having to shoot at anyone."

"Is it a requirement to be a chauvinist when you work for Hank?" She winked.

"You wouldn't want us any other way." He didn't care how he sounded. Women were more than capable to be police officers, in the military, and on the front line. He just didn't want his baby sister having to point a gun at someone. Or worse, get shot in the heat of the moment, like he did. She was a mother now.

"Here's to family." Serra raised her glass. "The ones we're born to and the ones we find along the way."

"I'll drink to that," he raised his glass.

Linc kissed Serra on the lips. Jax tried not to groan. Maybe after this trip to New York, he'd see if Serra had a friend. Nothing serious. Just someone to grab a coffee with. And sex. He wanted sex.

Pounding on the front door interrupted them and his errant thoughts about getting laid.

"You expecting someone?" Linc narrowed his eyes.

"Nope." He slid his chair back.

Since he was home, his gun was locked in the safe. His house was on several acres. His neighbors had as much land or more. The house couldn't be seen from the street. He'd been meaning to get a dog. If he had a bad-ass German Shepherd, he wouldn't need to grab his gun to greet an uninvited guest.

"I'll be right back." Never can be too careful. He'd met a lot of shady people in his career.

Linc stood too. "I have mine. We'll go to the door together."

Serra's eyes grew wide. "What is it?"

"Nothing, sweetheart. Just being cautious. Sit tight." Linc gripped Serra's shoulder.

"You two are scaring the shit out of me."

"We're just being practical," he said.

"You're being paranoid. Like usual." She shook her head.

The pounding grew more urgent. He might have agreed with her before the continued pounding. Whoever was at his door needed to get in. If it was one of his siblings in distress, they would have walked right in or called on the phone. His friends were all in the Brotherhood. They too would have called in an emergency. No one he knew would just show up and pound on his door. And he was pretty sure the little girls selling cookies didn't knock like that either.

He didn't have to tell Linc to cover him. They'd been a

team for years. Together, they went to the door. He peered through the peep-hole. Nothing.

"Who's there?" He turned to Linc and shrugged.

Linc flipped up the strap of his holster and nodded.

The knocking continued, but it seemed lower on the door.

"Step away from the door so I can see you." It was an order he hoped this person would follow.

"Ajax?" A small voice drifted through the wood.

"Did you hear that?" he whispered to Linc.

Linc tapped his ear and shook his head. The ringing must be in over drive today.

He had heard that small voice before. A voice that used his given name. Other than his mother and sister, not too many people ever called him Ajax. His stomach twisted. Who was playing him?

"Take aim." He whispered again, but made sure Linc could read his lips.

Linc drew his gun.

"Who's out there? Show yourself now or I'm going to blow your head off."

The knocking stopped.

He checked the peep-hole. Something moved to his right. The person stepped back on his stoop which allowed the front lights to spill over them. Not them. Her. A woman. She teetered on her feet and held out her arms to steady herself. He wasn't sure, but her face looked banged up. He squinted to get a better look. The blood drained from his head. She wasn't any woman. She had been his woman in another lifetime.

"Put your weapon away." He held a hand up to Linc and tugged open the door.

The cold air hit him first. The blood on her face knocked him off-balance. She stumbled forward. He caught her.

"Help me."

CHAPTER 3

Jax scooped Eden into his arms and carried her inside. She rested her head on his shoulder and closed her eyes. The right one was swollen and red. Someone had popped her good. Probably her husband or boyfriend. Bastard. Blood had run from her lip and dried over her chin. A hand-print covered her cheek. He tried to ignore the urge to snap the neck of whoever did this. She wasn't his any longer. He wouldn't get involved other than to get her cleaned up and to the hospital where she could make a report.

He placed her on the sofa. "Eden, who did this to you?" What was she doing here? That should be his first question.

"What is going on?" Serra ran into the room and stopped short. "Oh. Let me get some ice."

Eden stared at him with one wide eye. "I didn't know where else to go." Her voice shook.

"The police would have been a good start." He squatted down in front of her.

Tears ran down her cheeks. She shook her head and wrung her hands in her lap. "I can't go to them. I'm not safe."

Lincoln came into the room. "I checked outside. Nothing out of the ordinary. Eden, is that your silver Civic out on the street?"

Eden nodded and more tears fell. "Hi, Linc."

"Hi." Linc ducked his head.

"Did anyone follow you?" Jax asked. After all these years, she showed up and probably brought a world of drama with her.

"I don't think so." She kept her gaze on her hands.

"Here's the ice." Serra handed the plastic bag to him.

"Let's give them a minute." Lincoln took Serra out into the kitchen.

He held the ice to the side of her face. She winced. "Keep it there. Did your husband do this to you? You can file domestic abuse charges. I'll take you to the station." He stood.

She gripped his wrist. Her nails dug into his skin. "No. I don't have a husband. My cousin John did this. I can't go to the police since the entire department will be on his side. He wanted to prove a point."

"Looks like he did." When he saw John King, he'd ring the shithead's neck until it snapped in half.

"He wants something I have and I won't give it to him. I need to get to New York. Can you take me?" She tilted her chin up and met his gaze. Her lip quivered.

For fuck's sake. He could never handle a crying

woman. And Eden never cried in front of him. She kept her emotions tucked in close. At least she used to. When her emotions threatened to boil over and scald her, she ran. He often saw her retreating back in his dreams.

"You come here after all this time and ask me for help? You've got some balls, lady. I'll give you that." He paced the room. Confusion burrowed through his head and right down to the wound in his heart.

"I know I have no right. I wouldn't blame you for saying no. I probably would if I were you, but I have nowhere to turn. There is no one I can trust."

"Why do you think you can trust me?"

She pressed her lips together. "You are the most honest person I've ever met."

"Lucky me."

"I'm so sorry for what I did. I was a coward and I'm probably being a coward now. If my cousin hadn't gone crazy on me, I wouldn't even be here. But he's threatened to kill me in twenty-four hours if I don't give him what he wants. I'm pretty sure he'll do it."

"What are you involved in, and how dare you drag me into it?" His heart yelled for him to shut the fuck up and hold her in his arms until she felt safe. His head screamed for him to throw her ass out on the porch. He didn't want any part of her troubles.

"I have proof that's going to send his father to jail." She wiped her nose with the back of her hand. "Do you have a tissue?"

"I'll be right back." He marched into the bathroom and yanked some toilet paper off the roll.

Lincoln intercepted him on the way out. "What's going on?"

"I have no clue. She says she wants my help."

"Do you want me to interrogate her?"

"I can handle her. I'll probably drop her at the police station once she's calmed down some."

"Are you sure you're okay with her here?"

He had no idea if he was okay. He'd sworn to himself he never wanted to lay eyes on Eden King again. She'd broken his heart in so many pieces he wasn't sure he'd found them all to put himself back together again. At the same time, he never stopped loving her. He was pretty fucked up where she was concerned. "You and Serra can get out of here. You don't need to get tangled up in this mess. I'll see you when I get back."

"Hell no, brother. I'm staying put. We'll hang out in the back room. Even if the only thing you do for her is take her to the station, I'm coming with you."

"Thanks for having my back."

"That's what partners are for." Linc slapped him on the shoulder.

He returned to Eden in his living room. "Here." He handed her the toilet paper he'd wadded in his hand.

"Thanks."

"Does your proof have something to do with your uncle being accused of raping that woman when he was in college?" He dropped down on the sofa next to her and ran a hand through his hair to avoid touching her.

"You know about it?"

"I don't live under a rock." Thought at the moment he kind of wished he did.

"I didn't say that."

"You don't have to." He knew how she felt about him.

"Jax, what happened between us–"

"Please, don't. I don't want to talk about the past."

"You never wanted to talk about anything."

"I believe that was you." He had talked more than he ever had in his life where she was concerned.

He begged her, in fact. Heat filled his face remembering the hot tears pouring down his face while he asked her to stay in the hospital with him and hold his hand. His leg had hurt so much he could not stand the burning pain running up and down his shin and thigh. He had been afraid and didn't want to be left alone, but she had gone without a look back.

"I'm sorry I couldn't be what you wanted." She wiped her nose with the toilet paper and winced.

She had been everything he wanted. Well, he also wanted her to be his wife and the mother of his children, but that plan had been pulled from his grasp when they lost the baby. She had been relieved. He had been angry.

"Looks like your career is getting you into trouble again."

"I have to report the truth."

"You could walk away from this one. Save your life."

"You're asking me to bury what I know? Absolutely not. I don't care that he's my uncle. The truth must come out and rectify what's happened to this woman. He can't be allowed to get away with what he did and then sit on the highest court in the land passing judgement on other people. I won't back down. I just need a way to get to New York so my cousin can't find me. Please help me. You're the best. I've followed your career."

"You kept tabs on me?" The ice around his heart melted some, and the anger burned his veins at the same time. This woman had done nothing but wreak havoc on him.

She smiled for the first time. "I wanted to know you were okay and happy."

"And your job let you do that." Had she been happy? Did she miss what they had the way he had missed her?

"There are some perks to being an investigative reporter."

"Getting your ass kicked isn't one of them."

"I guess I deserve that." She leaned her head back against the couch. "I'm so tired and every part of my body hurts. I might have bruised ribs. John trampled all over me."

"He won't get away with it."

"Oh yeah? Who's going to stop him? You and Linc?"

"He can't have friends in every part of the department. I can call my boss and get you someone to trust. You can file a report against him."

"I won't be safe and you know it. Even if one person believes me, once the story hits, he's going to come after me. I'll ruin his father and my family name. Please. I just need a ride to New York. I'll pay you."

"Just like that. I'm supposed to be your Uber driver halfway across the country as if we never had a past and then forget I ever saw you all so you can get the headline?"

"I don't have anywhere else to go."

Dark circles covered her eyes. The swollen one grew uglier. He reached over and placed the ice against the bruise.

Her forehead had a gash in it and her lip was cracked. She was still beautiful with her light brown hair in waves around her face. "You're missing an earring." He pointed.

She grabbed at her ears. "Those were my favorites. Damn. Anyway, what do you say, Ajax? Please."

Jesus, when she used his full name, his belly grew hot. He had always loved the sound of his name on her lips. If she hadn't stood on his porch beaten and battered, he could have turned her away without a second thought. "You have no right to show up here and ask for my help after you left me when I needed you most." The hot sting of tears burned behind his eyes. He was a wuss and needed to get his shit together.

"I know. I was awful to you. I'm so sorry. You don't have to forgive me. I don't deserve it. I was frightened when you got shot. It's no excuse, but I couldn't handle watching you in that hospital bed. Not after what we'd been through."

"I needed you. I was dying inside because of the baby. No one else could understand how I felt, and then after I'd been shot..." He couldn't go on. The hurt tightened his chest and stole his breath.

"I'm so sorry." Her words were a whisper. "I should have apologized sooner, but I didn't think you ever wanted to see me again and I didn't blame you."

He had waited seven years for her to show up and say she was sorry. Sorry for leaving him. Sorry for not wanting to have a big family with him. Now here she was, beaten up and sitting on his couch. Was she really sorry or was it just the recent turn of events?

"As long as I didn't see you, I could get on with my life. I had to."

"Please take me to New York. I'll never bother you again. You'll be able to go back to your life."

"And what if I can't?"

CHAPTER 4

EDEN STILL LOVED JAX. That was the simple truth. A truth she had to keep to herself because he deserved better than hearing about her feelings. She'd broken his heart and she had no excuse except that fear had strangled her to within an inch of her life. Much like her cousin made her feel tonight. She had been with other men, but more for something to do than for anything real. She didn't believe in loving more than one person in a lifetime. Too bad she hadn't realized that before she left Jax.

She wanted to run her touch over Jax's strong arms and feel the flex of his muscles against her fingers, but she clasped her hands together instead. He had grown out his buzz cut. Now his shiny, black hair was long enough she could run her fingers through it. Which she had no intention of doing. His smooth, mocha colored skin made her insides sizzle. He was dark and strong with eyes the color of coffee that saw the truth even when it was hidden deep.

"I should go." She pushed off the couch and her body

protested in response, but she bit back the groan. "I'm sorry I came here. I shouldn't have. Say goodbye to Lincoln for me."

She hadn't thought about what she was doing when she got in the car. Logic had evaded her as she ran to the one person who had the power to keep her safe. He had always been her protector and she could trust him. He had never let her down unlike the way she let him down over and over. She'd find another way to get to New York. If she left now, John might not find her and once the story went live, he'd be foolish to kill her. Someone would notice. Wouldn't they?

"Wait." His deep voice grounded her in her spot.

She kept her back to him, not daring to turn around. If she saw the possibility in his eyes that he might help her, she'd fall to pieces. She wanted him to hold her right now and tell her she'd be okay. In his arms, no one would hurt her and she hurt so badly at the moment.

"Eden, look at me."

She turned, squared her shoulders, and met his gaze.

"Did you tell anyone you were coming here?"

"No."

"What's in New York?"

He was caving, and a sliver of hope held her head up. "I have a mini VHS tape with footage from the night in question locked away in a safe."

"In New York?" He raised his eyebrows.

"It was a stupid idea. I realize that now."

He rubbed a hand over his chin. "I have to make some arrangements and I only have five days. There's some-place I have to be after that."

"We can drive to New York in less than five days."

"We won't drive the whole way. I'll figure out the logistics, but after five days, if we're not there you're on your own. I can't miss my appointment for anything. Do you understand?"

"Yes." She wouldn't let him down this time. "I'll do whatever you say."

"Good. And after I get you to your tape, I want you to go away and never come back. No matter what happens."

He would never forgive her. Her heart ached for what she lost, but she deserved it. "I promise." She choked on the words.

"I can't believe I'm agreeing to this." He shook his head. "Do you want to get cleaned up while I make a call?"

"That would be great. Thank you, Ajax. I appreciate it."

"Just Jax."

"I don't understand. I always called you Ajax. You used to like it."

"That was before. Just Jax now."

"Sure." She would respect his boundaries. He was doing her a favor.

"The full bathroom is at the top of the stairs. You can run a bath if you want. Towels and ibuprofen are in the closet. I'll bring you a change of clothes. You're going to need to get out of those." He pointed at her.

Blood stained her top in a tie-died pattern. His thoughtfulness might kill her, but that was Jax. He thought of everything. That had been the quality that made him such a good cop and she suspected what made him a good bodyguard now. The reason he got shot that night was because his mind wasn't on his work. She had made him lose his focus because she'd lost their baby.

"You keep women's clothes handy?" She didn't want to wear another woman's clothing. Especially not a woman who had lain beside him in his bed.

"What? Oh, no." His smile tweaked out of the corners of his mouth, but it disappeared. "You'll have to wear something of mine."

Worse. She'd have the scent of him against her skin. "That would be great. Thanks. When will we leave? I want to break the story as quickly as possible before my cousin finds me."

"He's always going to look for you if you have the proof to ruin his father. You may never be safe. You do realize that, don't you?"

"My job is dangerous at times."

"And you were always willing to risk your safety for the job."

"Jax, I didn't mean for it to happen. Why can't you stay away from that? It wasn't my fault." The sob stuck in her throat.

"You never wanted a family."

"I wouldn't hurt our baby to get out of it." If she could make him understand, maybe some of the guilt would go away.

"But you weren't willing to stay home either."

"Neither were you." She had begged him not to go on that call. He'd been crazed at the hospital when he learned the baby was gone.

"You've got me there, lady. I lost a lot that night. More than you."

"Don't you dare tell me about my loss." Her voice shook, but she would not cry.

He cleared the space between them. His gaze burned through her. "You left me in that hospital room. I came home and your stuff was gone with nothing left except a note. A fucking note, Eden."

"I'm so sorry." She couldn't meet his gaze any longer. He was right. The tears threatened to betray her. "Never mind with helping me. I really should go." She turned.

He grabbed her arm and turned her back. "Stay. I'm being an ass. I'm sorry. The past is the past. We just weren't meant to be, and you had tried to tell me that a thousand times. I should have listened sooner." He released her and stepped away.

She missed his touch immediately. He was so wrong. He'd been her soul mate, but she had been too afraid to admit it back then. "We only have to be together for five days. I'm sure we can handle it. We're adults."

"Yeah, sure. Head upstairs. I'll bring the clothes." He pulled his phone from his pocket and turned his back to her. "Hank, it's Jax. I need a few favors. No, it's not about that." His voice drifted away as he went into the other room leaving her alone.

The only thing she was sure of was the need to reveal the evidence that proved her uncle had raped a woman. She wasn't sure how she would survive five days with Jax because she suspected she'd never want to leave him again after their time together.

Well, she'd have to forget about wanting him. Ajax may have loved her once, but she had nailed that coffin shut all by herself. When she had a goal, she usually met it. Losing Jax had been one of them.

He told her that night in the hospital he would hate her forever.

Jax was good at meeting goals too.

CHAPTER 5

"You'll get on the train in Shelby, and someone will pick you up in Minnesota. I haven't decided who's available yet, but I'm sending the tickets to Linc. I don't want anything tied to you. You'll be on the train for twenty-four hours," Hank Patterson said through the phone.

Hank was the best boss Jax ever had. He ran the Brotherhood Protectors like a tight ship, took no one's shit, expected the best, but was always there for his employees, no questions asked. They were more like a family. Hank had helped Lincoln hide Serra last winter and now Hank was helping him take Eden on the run. He hoped he didn't regret this.

"Thanks, Hank. Appreciate it."

"Keep your head on straight. I don't want you getting hurt."

"Yes, sir."

Hank knew about Eden and all that had happened between them. After he'd been shot, he was put on desk duty no longer able to be on the SWAT team. Hank came and recruited him for the Brotherhood. Hank expected complete honesty. He told Hank everything.

He ended the call and found Linc standing behind him in the kitchen. "You sure you want to do this?"

"You heard?"

"Hank sent me the case notes while he was talking to you. I'm your ride to the train station."

"You don't have to do that. I can get us there." He shoved his phone in his pocket.

"Safer if I take you. No trail. Eventually, this cousin will realize Eden came to you. They'll be looking for you too. I'm going to move Eden's car now and take Serra home. Then I'll be back to keep watch during the night. We leave first thing in the morning."

"Linc,-"

Linc put a hand up to stop him. "No explanations needed. We're brothers. I'll do anything for you."

"Even if you don't agree with me?"

"None of my fucking business what you do. I just want you to come back in one piece. I can keep you safe on this end, and Hank will take care of the rest. Get to New York, drop her wherever she needs to go, and sit in on your parole hearing. Easy."

If only it were that easy. How was he going to leave her on a sidewalk in New York City and drive away as if she hadn't shown up on his doorstep beaten and hurt? And when she put her life on the line by releasing the information against her uncle, he'd want to be there to make sure her fucking cousin didn't come looking for her. Shit, all he wanted to do was hold her in his arms and tell her he'd keep her safe. He almost forgot about their past when he saw her tonight. Almost.

"I owe you." He held Linc's gaze.

"Bullshit. You owe me nothing. I'll be back in an hour. We leave for the train around eight. Try and get some sleep tonight."

"I can stay up with you."

"I know you can, but you're going to be the only eyes on for a while after I drop you off. I want you to try and sleep now."

He was never going to be able to sleep with Eden in the next room. "See you in an hour. Thank Serra for cleaning up the kitchen."

"That was me."

"Yeah, right." He laughed. "Thanks, man. For everything."

He waited for Linc and Serra to leave before he headed upstairs to find clothes for Eden. He stood outside the bathroom door holding his T-shirt and sweatpants unsure of what to do. Probably should have had Serra bring these in. He had no desire to see Eden naked in his tub. Okay, maybe a little.

He knocked. "Eden? Can I come in?"

"Just a second," she said.

The lock clicked, and she opened the door. Her skin had a pink glow from the hot water that made his mouth run dry. Small droplets glistened against her shoulders mocking him from their place because his lips had been there on many nights. Her lip and eye were still swollen, but with the blood gone she looked more like herself. His black towel covered everything he'd had the privilege of seeing once and still could if he closed his eyes, which he was not about to do then and there.

"Here." He handed over the clothes.

Her fingers grazed his as she grabbed for them. The touch seared his skin. She could always make him hot with nothing more than a smile and a wink. He wished his brain would forget that.

"Thank you." She held his gaze.

"You can sleep in the guest room. We leave at eight." He turned to go afraid he might reach out and remove that damn towel.

"Wait."

"Eden, if you want to talk, please get dressed first."

She glanced down as if she didn't remember she was half-naked in front of him. Red blotches bloomed on her cheeks. At least this was uncomfortable for her too. He assumed.

"Can we go back to my place so I can pack a few things? In my hurry to get here, I didn't grab anything. I'll need stuff if I'm going to be gone for five days."

"Write a list. I'll send Linc."

She raised her eyebrows. "I'd rather not have your partner rummage through my underwear draw."

Truth be told, neither did he. "Write the list and I'll go when Linc gets back in an hour. I've seen your underwear."

"I bought new stuff after we broke up. So, no. I'm going to go with you. It will be quicker if I grab what I need instead of trying to explain where everything is. I also want my computer."

"No computer. Please get dressed. I'll be downstairs."

As much as he wanted to stand there and take in her beauty, he needed to walk away.

"Why can't I have my computer?" She yelled after his back.

"I'll be in the kitchen with a beer. You want one?" He kept moving.

She closed the door with force. He smiled. Good, she was flustered too even if it was only with his insisting she follow his rules. Because she'd have to if they were going to stay ahead of her cousin.

The King family had connections, money, and power. Societal rules didn't apply to her uncles and their children. Only Eden's dad seemed to not take advantage of his privileged life as much as the others.

Jax grabbed two beers from the fridge and a glass for Eden but put it back. Maybe she drank from the bottle now, and if she still preferred a glass, he didn't want her thinking he had remembered. Childish, but he couldn't help himself at the moment.

He didn't like the idea of her running with this story. Of course, justice should be served, but he wanted someone else on the front line. Thomas King would wipe the floor with anyone who tried to stop him. John King would help his father in any way possible. Eden would not be safe. The King men would hunt her down until something happened to her permanently. She was making a mistake by going after her uncle. Jax wanted to talk her out of her mission. Maybe convince her to give the story to someone else. She would never agree to that. Not the very driven Eden King. He could still try.

"Why can't I have my computer?" Eden stepped into the kitchen wearing his clothes.

His breath caught in his throat. His shirt hung off her bare shoulder, and she had tied the end into a knot at her waist. Her breasts pressed against the fabric, and all his heat ran south. She had rolled up his sweatpants probably so they wouldn't drag on the floor and revealed red painted toes. He loved the color red against her creamy skin.

"Jax, are you going to answer me?" She fisted her hands on her hips with a dare in her eyes.

He took a deep breath. "Sorry. Want one?" He held up the beer.

"Sure. Thanks."

He made sure not to touch her when he handed the bottle over. "Your IP address can be tracked if you hit the internet. I don't want anyone identifying our location. No one can know where you are or how we're traveling. In fact, we're taking a train because we won't need to show ID."

"A train? Are you kidding me? It will take forever to get to New York by train. I thought you only had five days. Do you have a glass?"

He pulled it back out of the cabinet and slid the glass across the counter. "The first leg of the route will be on the train. The ride will last about twenty-four hours. A sleeper cabin was booked in a Brotherhood Protector name that can't be traced. We get off in Minnesota where someone from the Brotherhood will meet us and take us to our next stop. We'll drive some of the way, and in

Chicago we'll hop a private plane where we won't be recorded as passengers."

"So, we'd better not go down like they did in that movie with the very hot Idris Elba."

"I don't know what you're talking about." He didn't like her thinking about other men as hot. Again, childish and again, he could not stop himself. At least he didn't say it out loud.

She smirked. "You still don't like to watch movies. You have this whole trip figured out already. That is just like you."

"We don't know each other anymore." And it was in his best interest not to get to know her any better. He couldn't afford to risk his heart with her. Not again. She could never be able to break his heart again.

"I want my computer."

"I don't care. You can't bring it. And where's your phone?" He should have thought of that sooner. He couldn't afford to lose focus either. He would keep her safe because he loved her once then send her on her way.

"In my car, I think."

He shot Linc a fast text to check and turn it off. "No phone. You can get a disposable one along the way, but you can't tell anyone where you are. Can I trust you?" Famous last words.

"I just want to get to New York."

"What are you going to do after your story hits? How are you going to stay safe?"

"I don't know. I haven't thought that far ahead. That's more your thing. The paper might be able to hire me a bodyguard for a while, until the news dies down. In a week, no one will even remember about the story."

"Your uncle is never going to forget. You will have ruined his life. You need a plan so he doesn't drive you off the road someday."

"You're being paranoid."

"I'm being practical. Your cousin beat the shit out of you a few hours ago and that had you running to me. I think you might want to pay attention to what I'm saying or find someone else to babysit you."

She put the untouched bottle on the counter. "You're right. I'm sorry. I'm going to get some sleep."

"I'm right?"

She met his gaze. "Yes, Ajax, you're right. I need to listen to you if I'm going to get to New York in one piece. I should have listened to you a long time ago, but I have to live with that, don't I?"

He stared at her unsure if he heard her correctly. "I don't want to be right. I want the last seven years back."

"For what? To fight with me through? We wanted different things back then, and a baby wasn't going to change that. Maybe Mother Nature knew what she was doing and spared us a lot of heartache."

"I thought that baby would be an adventure." He peeled the label on the beer bottle.

"Because that's how you see the world. A baby would have meant sacrifices."

"And you weren't ready to make those sacrifices. You didn't want to build a family with me." He leaned against the counter wanting to derail the conversation, but couldn't seem to keep his mouth shut.

"I was twenty-eight. My career was just taking off. Why shouldn't I have had the chance to make something of myself?"

"It's always you and your career."

"And you and yours. I never stopped you from being on the SWAT team."

He pushed away from the counter. "No, you just ran away when I got hurt." His voice shook. He should back down, but he stood his full height.

"I was afraid you'd die." She yelled. "I didn't want to be the wife of a SWAT team officer who ran into trouble headfirst all the time. And I didn't want a huge family I'd have to take care of by myself if you didn't come home."

"What about now? What do you want now?"

"I only want to get to New York and run with my story."

Her honest answer dumped cold water on his head. He turned away from her and stared out the window into the dark night.

She gripped his arm. "Jax, I'm sorry. I don't want to fight with you. You're doing me a favor. Can we please table the past for the next five days? After New York, you can go on with your life, and I'll never bother you again."

He looked down at her. He always loved her petite frame against him. She stared back with wide, expectant deep blue eyes he could drown in. Her hair curled around her face and hung past her shoulders. He wanted to tangle his fingers through every strand. His heart knocked against his ribs.

She leaned up and placed a soft kiss on his cheek. Her lips were cool against his heated skin, and her soapy smell intoxicated him. He didn't think. He grabbed her by the shoulders and kissed her full on the mouth.

She stiffened in his grip, but before he could let her go, she surrendered and kissed him back. His heart banged louder, but his brain yelled for him to stop before this went any further. Instead, he ran his hands down her back and cupped her bottom.

He'd missed her so much. Sometimes the hurt was so bad it would stop him from breathing.

Her hands found the bottom of his shirt and her fingers played against his skin. Were they really doing this? Now? He needed to focus before he fucked everything up.

He eased back. "Eden, we should–"

The front door opened. They jumped apart. She wiped her mouth with the back of her hand and winced as she passed over the cut. He tugged his shirt into place and ran a hand over his hair.

Lincoln had returned.

"Good night." She slipped from the kitchen before they were caught, but she had to pass Linc on her way upstairs.

Lincoln stood in the doorway with eyebrows raised and a duffle over his shoulder.

He downed the rest of his beer and said, "Don't ask."

CHAPTER 6

Eden stretched in Jax's bed. Well, Jax's guest bed. A chill hovered around the guest room as if to push her away because she had no business in Jax's house, but the soft down comforter wrapped her in warmth telling her stay. Her muscles ached. She wished her body hurt for reasons other than her cousin pounding on her, reasons like Jax making love to her all night, but that wish would never come true, no matter how hot their kiss had been.

She couldn't believe John had beaten her up. Her uncle may be powerful, but they were tight. That could not be true any longer, if it ever was. No family existed for her any longer. She would be alone now.

She dragged herself from the bed still wearing Jax's clothes. They smelled fresh and cottony, like him. She needed to get into something of her own or lose her mind. How was she going to handle five days with him?

She made the bed as a small gesture of appreciation for Jax opening his home to her. The décor was cozy with beige walls and dark carpet. A rocking chair offered a place to sit and take in the view of the mountains as the sun peaked over their tops. A nice room for a nursery. She sucked in a breath and chased that thought away before it took hold. It might be early, but she wanted to get out of there.

The kitchen was still dark, and the coffee maker was off. Lincoln snored on the couch. Jax must still be asleep. They were safe. For now, but would John find them? Would her uncle send reinforcements?

She rummaged through the drawers and cabinets until she found what she needed. She'd make Jax a cup too. He always liked his coffee with a little milk. The memory tugged a smile from her lips. Best not to think about the memories of waking up with him.

The back door opened and she jumped. "You scared me."

Jax brought in the cold spring air. "Sorry. I loaded my suitcase into Linc's vehicle." He took the mug from her hand. "We can get coffee on the way. You wanted to stop at your house first, so we need to hit the road soon. Is Sleeping Beauty still out?"

"I'm right here, smart ass." Lincoln wiped a hand over his stubble. His T-shirt and jeans were wrinkled, but his eyes held the look of confidence and control. "I need five minutes. Good morning, Eden."

"Morning."

Lincoln handed her a small duffle bag. "Serra took the liberty of purchasing a few things for you. Enough clothes for a week, toiletries, things like that. I hope you don't mind, but she assumed you didn't want to be stuck wearing Jax's clothes. She had been in a similar situation not all that long ago and didn't appreciate going out in public in my jeans."

"That was thoughtful. Thank you and please thank her too." She ran into the bathroom and swapped the over-sized sweats for a pair of black flared yoga pants and a long, cozy, brushed sweatshirt that fit perfectly.

She didn't have a lot of time for girlfriends and was flooded by the high spirits Serra's gift gave her. When all this was over, she'd thank Serra properly. She stuffed Jax's things in his hamper and grabbed the duffel.

The men waited for her outside. Lincoln's big, black truck smelled new and leathery. She inhaled until her lungs were full. She hadn't purchased a car in nine years. Jax took the seat up front and punched her address into the GPS.

"You know where I live?" Her voice climbed with excitement. He'd been keeping tabs on her.

"I ran a full profile on you last night," Lincoln said pulling out of the driveway.

So much for fantasies of Jax missing her.

They made it to her town in record time. The GPS lady told Lincoln to take the next turn. He made the left and came to a halt. Police cars and fire trucks blocked their path.

"Is that my house?" She reached for the door.

"Don't move." Jax yelled.

She jumped as if the door handle were hot. "I need to get to my house."

"Let me check it out first." Jax bounded from the truck.

"Don't do it, Eden." Lincoln glared at her.

"I have to."

"Jax needs to protect you, and he can't do it if you run off half-cocked. Stay put with me."

"Sorry." She ran before he could say another word. She doubted he'd shoot her.

She pushed through the crowd of first responders and tried to get to her house. Her two sets of neighbors stood on the sidewalk and gawked. Thick smoke spread into the air. Flames licked the roof of her house like a dragon trying to fight its way out. She covered her nose with the collar of her shirt because even at a safe distance the smoke wanted to coat her lungs. Tears stung her eyes. The damage had been done. She'd never be able to save her home.

Someone grabbed her arm and yanked her back. Her head whipped around.

"Eden, what are you doing here? I thought you were dead." Emma Martin dragged her away from the crowd and behind a row of hedges out of sight of the crowd.

"Emma, I don't have time for this. I need to see what's happening." She tried to pull away from Emma's vice-like grip around her wrist, but she couldn't.

Emma stared at her with wide, brown eyes. "I saw you hadn't come in to work today, and everyone was wondering why. It's not like you not to check in with your latest story then I heard about the fire on the police scanner in our department. I came to see if you were okay."

"I'm fine. Now let me go." She tugged again, but Emma wasn't having any of it. She should be grateful someone cared enough to check on her, especially a friend from work, but she didn't have time for gratitude.

"You can't get any closer. There's a body in the house. The police chief is calling the county prosecutor. If that body isn't you, then you're going to be questioned. What happened, Eden?" Emma stepped back and let her go.

"Does anyone from the paper know you're here?"

"I ran out without saying anything. I was in such a panic when I heard your address. I didn't even think first. I just took off. Are you involved in something dangerous?"

"Don't tell anyone that you saw me." She didn't want her whereabouts given away. They needed as much time as possible to get to New York ahead of John and her uncle. And she didn't want anyone to hurt Emma. If John suspected Emma knew where she was, he'd kill her.

"There you are." Jax hurried over to her. "We have to go."

"Who are you?" Emma narrowed her eyes.

"I'm her bodyguard. Who are you?"

"She works with me. There's a body in my house. He's setting me up."

"Who is?" Emma asked.

"Eden, now We need to leave."

"Are you in trouble?" Emma said.

"I am. I didn't hurt that person in my house. I hope you can believe that. I have a story that's going to mess up a lot of lives, and the people involved don't want me to tell it. Please don't tell anyone you saw us. Can you do that, Emma?"

"If this is about a story, I won't say a word. You need to

get out of here, then. Get someplace safe and break the news. That's what we do." Emma hugged her and slipped into the crowd again.

"Let's go." Jax grabbed her hand and ran back to Lincoln waiting at the end of the street.

Lincoln threw the truck in reverse. She turned to see out the back window. She'd bought that house after she'd been on the road investigating women's issues for a year. After Jax was shot, she couldn't bear to be in Montana and took an assignment that brought her overseas. Even the borders of the US seemed to close in around her back then. The only way to get over losing the baby and losing Jax was to put thousands of miles between her and him. It took the full year before she could step foot in Montana and still breathe. She had found a place an hour from Jax, and now that place was burning embers. She would destroy her uncle before he hurt her anymore.

Lincoln drove farther and farther away until only the trail of black smoke blew into the sky. Jax turned in his seat and grabbed her hand.

"Babe, I'm sorry about the house. You can't trust anyone. Not even people you work with. You need to trust me now."

"Everything I own is in that house. Was in that house. What am I supposed to do?"

"Do you still want to go to New York? I can drop you somewhere else if you want to forget the story."

"Are you kidding me? After what that bastard just did? Do you really think I'm going to let that lie now? No fucking way."

"Eden, your mouth." Jax dropped her hand.

He always hated when she cursed. "What? You've never heard a woman say fuck before? Fuck, Ajax. I think it's appropriate at the moment." She crossed her arms over her chest.

Pictures of her and her dad were gone. She had kept old photo albums of when she and Jax were together. Those would be ruined too. And the awards she received for journalism. And of course, her computer, with everything she'd ever written, would be a melted mess.

"Linc, I need you to find out who was in that house. They're going to try and pin this on her."

"I'll get on it right away."

Lincoln pulled into the Shelby train station with its one-story wood board building and parked alongside the curb. "We weren't followed. Most likely whoever set the house on fire was long gone anyway."

"They weren't going to wait around to see if Eden showed up. They're hoping the cops find her and detain her," Jax said.

"Then she can't run with her story. Who's going to believe a criminal? But why would she burn down her own house?" Lincoln rummaged through the glove box.

"Because whoever is in there was murdered first."

"Could you two stop talking about me as if I'm not sitting back here?" She didn't mean to bite anyone's head off. "I'm sorry."

Lincoln ignored her and spoke to Jax. "I'll do some investigating on the Jane Doe in the house. Or John Doe. You can slip inside the train and not be noticed. Here are your tickets. The train arrives in ten minutes. Hank booked sleeper service for you. You can hide out all night.

At least for the next twenty-four hours you'll be safe. Good luck, bro."

The men shook hands. She and Jax walked across the wood planks that acted as the walkway over the tracks and waited by the bench.

The heat of embarrassment burned her cheeks. She had kick dropped herself right into the middle of this mess and managed to drag Jax along too. Meeting his gaze at the moment was like staring into the sun. She couldn't do it.

"I'm sorry about your house. I'll help you with the insurance company when I get back if you want."

She should have been more appreciative of him when they were together. He always made sure he took care of her.

"Jax–" Her words caught in her throat. She had to try again. "Jax, I'm sorry for leaving you. I hope some day you can forgive me." She had never really meant to hurt him even though she'd left knowing that was exactly what her leaving would do. She'd beaten herself up over the years for taking the coward's way out. He had deserved honesty and she had been stingy with it. She didn't know how to make up for her bad choices then. If she could go back, she would do it all differently. The best gift she could give him now was to leave him alone.

He pressed his lips together. He looked down at her. His dark eyes were filled with hurt, and she wanted to make all the pain go away for him.

"Let's not talk about the past now. We can't change it anyway. But thanks for the apology. And I'm sorry too. I should have listened to you better. You never wanted a family. I thought I could change your mind."

"If the baby had made it–"

"We'd be divorced. You never wanted to be a cop's wife."

She had wanted to be Jax's wife, and she had hoped in time he would leave the force or retire early. He could have been anything he wanted, but that had been foolish thoughts on her part. How could she have asked him to leave the career he loved when she hadn't been willing to do the same?

The silver, double decker, train pulled into the station announcing its arrival with a strong blow of its whistle. The brakes breathed a sigh, and the train stopped. The conductors in their black hats and uniforms stepped off the train along with a few passengers lugging suitcases.

A man with his neck buried in the collar of his trench coat hurried onto the train ahead of them. She checked over her shoulder. Had John followed them even though Lincoln thought they were safe for now? After the story hit, she'd find a way to go underground so her uncle could never find her.

Jax grabbed her hand and she stopped short. He tugged her closer and whispered in her ear. "We will draw less attention if we act like we're together."

"Got it." She couldn't keep asking him to put himself in harm's way for her.

The train must make stops between there and Saint Paul. She'd get off in the middle of the night and save him from having to take care of her. She had been selfish again coming to him.

Jax flashed the tickets at the conductor.

"Right this way, sir. I'll show you to your bedroom where you can unpack and get comfortable before joining us in the lounge car or dining car for lunch."

They followed the conductor down a narrow hall, no wider than one person, with windows on one side to take in Big Sky country and the entry into the bedrooms on the other. She did not want to be confined to a train with Jax for twenty-four hours because she wasn't sure she could trust herself around him. She couldn't resist his kiss any more than she could hold her breath for more than thirty seconds. The decision was made. She'd wait for him to fall asleep, then sneak out and get off the train at the first opportunity. She'd find another way to New York.

Two young boys barreled up the hall from the other direction. They pushed and shoved each other into the wall of windows.

"Slow down, boys." The conductor blocked their path with his tall frame and wide shoulders. "You don't want to disturb the other guests."

They mumbled a few apologies and ran past as the conductor, she, and Jax turned sideways to clear the path.

"Tight fit," she said.

"It's close quarters here on the Prime Mover, but I think you'll be cozy enough." The conductor swung open the door and stepped aside for them to enter.

The space wasn't much bigger than a coffin. "Jax?" Sweat popped out on forehead and upper lip. She grabbed the wall for support. "Will we run out of oxygen in here?"

"It's okay, babe. We'll be fine." He kissed the top of her head. "My wife has a little claustrophobia."

Wife? She ignored the flutter in her stomach. He was acting, being her bodyguard. She shouldn't like the sound of that word coming from his lips.

"No need to explain, sir. You and the missus will be fine. You can place your suitcase up above the single seat. Do you need me to show you how to slide the bench down into a bed?"

"No, thank you. I've traveled this way before." Jax slipped him a folded bill.

She had no idea how much these tickets cost or how much that tip was. She owed him far more than she could ever repay him, but she would start with the monetary part first after she made it to New York.

Jax locked the door after the conductor and dropped onto the bench. He rubbed the spot above his knee.

"Does your leg still bother you?" She wanted to reach out and help him, but she stayed put.

That bench doubled as their bed. She bit her swollen lip and almost cried out. They'd have to share a bed or sleep sitting up.

"Only during the rainy season. Are you okay? You look like those bruises might be bothering you."

"All good."

He never told her how he really felt about anything and that had driven her mad. She could never really be close enough to him if he kept pushing her away. At least that's what she told herself when she packed her bags and left him.

"This room is tiny. Oh no, the toilet and the shower are in the same space." She was not about to use the bathroom with him only inches away from her. She'd hold it all night.

He laughed. "I've been in worse situations. At least it's clean, and the water is probably warm. My leg will appreciate that."

"I'll pay you back once I can access my bank accounts again." She sat down next to him and tried to ignore the way his solid thighs filled out his jeans. She turned her gaze out the window to the parking lot.

"Don't worry about the money. Are you holding up okay since we saw your house?"

A police car turned into the lot. The red and blue lights spun as the front end dipped and bobbed over the uneven pavement. "Jax, I think we have company." No time to answer his caring question.

He leaned over her to get a better look. "Shit."

"They're coming for me."

"We don't know that. There could be a wanted felon on the train too."

"Thank you for trying to make me feel better, but we both know that's not the truth. If this train doesn't pull out right now, the police could hold us up." Sweat ran between her breasts and down the back of her neck. She needed to cool down and tied her hair in a knot on the top of her head with the ponytail holder around her wrist.

"How did they know where we went?" Jax moved away and took his musky smell with him. "Linc said no one followed us, and I believe him. He's never wrong about that, and we were out of there before you were noticed. Did you tell your friend you were taking the train?"

"Why would I do that?"

"I don't know, Eden. Girls like to talk."

She wanted to slug him. "You can be so sexist sometimes."

"It's the alpha in me." He shot her a crooked smile.

She could never stay mad at him for long. "What do we do?"

He checked out the window, and she followed his gaze. The police cruiser had parked, but the cops hadn't come out of the vehicle. The train whistle blew and the train rolled forward like a big, metal feline on the prowl. The police still hadn't exited the car.

"What gives with those two?" She pointed out the window.

"False alarm. They're getting sent to another call. Maybe the body has been identified. I don't care as long as they don't stop this train."

The train hitched forward and picked up speed. Shelby and the police officers faded away. They were safe again. She let out a long breath.

He ran a hand over his face. "You hungry? I'm starving."

"Should we talk about us first?"

He stood. "Nothing to talk about. Let's go pretend to be man and wife in the dining car." He held out his strong, calloused hand.

She tilted her chin and met his gaze. "Ajax, we need to talk."

He grabbed her hand and pulled her up. "I don't want to talk, but you can keep calling me by my given name. You always had a way of making it sound sexy."

The dare in his eyes dried the words on her tongue.

Her feelings for him scared her because she had tucked them away in a tight, little corner of her heart, and by showing up at his doorstep and asking for his help, she'd cracked open that protected space.

"What about the body in my house? Am I going to get arrested for that?"

"I'll make some calls and find out what's going on. You're going to be questioned when they realize whoever it is, isn't you. Do you have a grudge against anyone? An old boyfriend maybe?"

She didn't want to imagine jealousy in his tone. "Nothing like that."

"So there hasn't been a guy in your past that did you wrong?"

"There hasn't been anyone in the past seven years I've cared that much about."

He turned his gaze toward the window. "I shouldn't be, but I'm glad to hear it."

"It's okay to still have feelings for me."

"No, it isn't."

CHAPTER 7

JAX PAID the dinner bill and pushed out of the chair. The dining car was full of people clanking forks and knives and laughing over their food. The train hurried on through Big Sky Country on its way to Minnesota in the morning, but only the reflection of the car came back at them in the oversized windows. Night had fallen and taken the view.

"Do you want to go back to the cabin?" He shoved his wallet in his front pocket.

He and Eden hadn't said much during dinner. He had kept his eyes on the passengers looking for something out of the ordinary, but everyone there was either on a business trip in their suits with their laptops out on the table or a family taking pictures on their phones, probably on vacation or their way home. He hadn't even seen the guy in the trench coat that boarded the train the same time as them.

"Can we sit in the lounge car for a little while? Maybe grab an after-dinner drink?"

He didn't know how to say no to her. That had been his big problem in the past. He'd been so in love with her and completely confused why a woman like Eden, with her family connections, smarts, beauty, and money, would want him. He had believed he was the luckiest son of a bitch on the planet. Maybe if he'd played it a little less desperate, she would have stayed. Or not.

He held out his hand. "I'd rather be in the cabin. No one will see us there."

"No one knows we're on this train."

"We don't know that for sure. And anyone can get on before St. Paul. I don't want to take any chances. We stay in the room until morning. We can grab a quick breakfast before we depart, but that's it."

She slid her soft hand into his. Acting like husband and wife gave him a good excuse to touch her.

"You are no fun, Jax Montero." Her blue eyes shone like sun glittering across a lake.

Maybe she didn't know how to say no to him now. Maybe they'd have a chance. He stopped short. Their chance was over. He would do well to remember that and to remember how he came home from the hospital to an empty house and a note. He dropped her hand.

"Let's go." He didn't wait to see if she followed and didn't care if the tightness in his voice gave him away. The train swayed under his feet as he pushed through the doors into the next car.

"Is something wrong?" She whispered behind him.

"I'm fine. Just tired." He skirted past the oversized club

chairs in the lounge car and through the next set of doors to the sleeper car.

"Don't do that." She grabbed his arm and stopped him in the narrow hallway near their room.

Passengers came up from the far end of the hall. They had to turn to their sides to let them pass.

"Evening," the man said. His wife and children were in tow.

Jax nodded.

"Good evening," Eden said. After the family passed, she continued. "Jax, please don't shut me out now."

He unlocked the cabin door and stepped aside to let her enter first. "I don't know what you're talking about." He locked the door behind them and kicked off his boots.

She pulled her hair from the rubber thing holding it back. Her blonde waves floated around her shoulders. A pink glow had crept into her cheeks and made his insides burn for her. He wanted nothing more than to pull her into his arms, but he had to fight the urge. She didn't want him as a man any longer. She wanted a bodyguard.

"Oh, please. You barely said a word during dinner. That nice man said hello to you, and you gave him that scowl of yours that has children and bunnies running. What's going on?"

He couldn't tell her the real reason for his foul mood was it hurt to be here with her, pretending, but knowing they would have to live separate lives. "I can keep you safe until I leave you in New York. I'm good at my job. You don't have to worry about that, but once we part ways, I don't know what will happen to you. Is your life really worth this story?" He wanted to convince her to give it up and save herself, but he never had that kind of power.

"My uncle doesn't deserve to be on the highest court in the land if he raped a woman." Her eyes blazed with anger.

"Have you seen the tape?" His leg complained about all the standing today. Most days he could forget about the gun shot wound, but on damp days so close to the parole hearing the ache seemed to take on a slow burn instead.

"Well, no, but why would she say he did it if he didn't?"

He pulled down the seats to make a bed and flopped onto the mattress. "Babe, people lie all the time for all the wrong reasons. I'm not saying she's making anything up, but if we found out she did, I wouldn't be anymore surprised than if she was telling the truth."

"I believe her and you should too."

"I believe the facts. But it's your story and there's nothing I can say to make you change your mind. What are you going to do when you break this wide open and your uncle turns up the screws? Because he will."

"I don't know yet. But I'll figure it out. Why are you going to New York? You never said."

"Parole hearing." He didn't want to say more.

"Who did you arrest in New York?"

"Does it matter?"

"Maybe."

"Why do you care, Eden?" He needed to control his emotions, but they slipped out of his grasp.

He went into survival mode when she showed up at his door, but now that it was a full day later, his leg hurt like a bitch, and he was trapped in a close space with the most beautiful woman he'd ever laid eyes on. He wanted to fight. She'd never given him that chance when she left.

"I don't know, Jax. Maybe I feel like I owe you."

Anger shot him off the bed. He stared down at her. "I don't want your fucking pity. I got on with my life after you left and I'm doing just fine without you. I'm not the one who showed up beaten and begging for help."

She flinched.

His dinner fought its way back up. "Eden, I'm–"

"Save it. I had it coming. I'm going to get ready for bed. Can you wait in the hallway while I use the bathroom? There's no privacy in this casket."

"Yeah. Sure." He closed the door behind him and leaned against it.

He acted like a fucking jerk. His pride was bruised, and he lashed out. If he was going to be honest, that was probably the real reason Eden had left him. He'd lashed out at her when the baby died and lashed out again while he lay broken in that hospital bed after he'd been shot.

The pain in his leg had choked the breath from him back then. He was angry and didn't know what to do with all of that ugliness coursing through his veins. She had been the closest target and he never missed a target.

He needed to stick to the plan. Get her to New York. Go to the parole hearing and go home. Maybe forget about Eden King finally.

The man from Shelby station came down the hall. He'd removed the trench coat, but wore a black suit and carried a tablet under his arm.

"Howdy," Jax said.

"Hello." The man nodded.

"You came on the train in Shelby with me and my wife." Something about this man made him take notice. Could be the scar on his neck or the blank look in the man's black eyes. Or it could just be years of training to suspect everyone.

The man stopped. "Really? I hadn't noticed anyone else getting on the train. Shelby is such a quiet stop. No one is ever there. Where you headed?"

How could the guy not have noticed? They were the only three getting on at a small, barely used station that didn't even house train representatives. "Taking this ride all the way to the end. It's our honeymoon. You?"

"Chicago. Business. Congratulations, then. I'm going to be getting on." He moved past Jax and turned at the other end of the hall.

The twist in his stomach told him to keep an eye out for that guy. There may be more to his story, or Jax was paranoid. Better safe than sorry.

Eden opened the door. "You can come back in."

She had swapped her clothes for his sweatshirt that hung to the middle of her bare thighs. The sight of her legs made his throat dry up. He brought shorts to sleep in, but he'd have to keep his jeans on because there was no way he'd survive brushing up against her skin.

He cleared his throat. "You can take the inside of the bed."

"Would you be more comfortable there?"

"I want to put myself between you and the door."

"That's very sweet of you."

"It's my job. Do you mind if I sleep without my shirt?" His core burned from desire and he needed air.

She dropped her gaze to the floor then brought it back up to meet his. "Whatever you want. Goodnight." She climbed into the bed and turned her back to him.

He tugged his shirt over his head then removed his gun and holster and placed them within reach on the floor under the bed. He lay down beside her, careful not to touch her. He stayed on his side, with his back to her, to give her space. "Goodnight."

The darkness and the rocking of the train did nothing to lull him to sleep. Instead, he listened to Eden's breathing deepen and inhaled her citrus scent. He shifted and tried to find a comfortable place for his aching leg, but no position eased the pain.

"Jax, you're fidgeting." Her voice was a whisper.

"I'm sorry. I can sleep in the chair."

She grabbed his arm. Her touch burned his skin. "No, I can. You'll be all cramped up like that."

"I'll be fine. I probably won't sleep much anyway. If I stay awake, I'll hear someone at the door."

She gripped his arm tighter. "Please don't get up."

"I'm going to keep you awake with my fidgeting, as you like to call it." He fought it, but a smile tugged at his lips. She had always called his restlessness at night fidgeting.

"Can you look at me?" She kept her voice low.

"It's kind of dark in here." He didn't need the light to see every inch of her. Her image had been burned onto his brain. He'd tried to forget her, but never could.

"Smart ass. Just face me."

He shifted again. "What's up?"

She placed a hand on his cheek. "It's always been you."

He grabbed her hand and placed it back on the mattress. "Don't do this, Eden. You're scared, and I'm familiar. Don't confuse that with something else."

She ran her fingers through his hair and sent chills down his back. He bit back a groan.

"I like your hair longer. And I'm not confusing anything. I've always loved you."

"But you left me."

"If I could do that over, I would. I'm so very sorry for hurting you at the worst possible time. I never stopped to think about how you lost that baby too. The grief crippled me, and I didn't expect it. I thought I'd be relieved to get on with my life, and I was devastated instead. Then not two days later, you ended up in the hospital almost dead. I couldn't handle it. I'm so sorry. I ruined everything."

He held his breath unsure if he should even move and end this moment. She said everything he'd wanted to hear all these years. He'd believed for so long that she hadn't grieved for their child or their relationship. He had spent a long time with a hole in his chest, and it wasn't until he could find purpose in his work again that he even started to heal.

Her fingers continued to comb through his hair. "Jax, please say something."

"If only you'd said all that then." Her touch drove him mad and still his hands stayed put.

"I didn't know how. I wanted to be mad at you for forcing me into a life I didn't want, but the truth is I did want that life, with you. Only I didn't know how much I wanted you until I was gone, and then I didn't have the right to ask you for forgiveness. I'm asking you now."

A fist closed around his throat. He swallowed. "I used to imagine you walking down the aisle to me. Then you told me you were pregnant, and I thought I had it all. I was so fucking sure of myself. I even bought you a ring. I wanted to get married before the baby came. That night, the night it happened, I was on my way home to propose when you called me." The darkness gave him cover and courage to share what he'd locked away.

He had blown his whole savings on that ring, but he wanted her to wear something she could be proud of around her family. He hadn't planned anything special except to make love to her beside the fire and ask her to be his wife. He had turned onto their street and his phone lit up with her number. Her voice was strangled with tears. He could barely understand her. Hospital had been the only word he needed.

"You never told me you bought a ring," she said on a long breath. "Twelve weeks. We were supposed to be safe that far along, but Mother Nature betrayed us."

"It wasn't meant to be. That's what you had said, and you were right."

"I was wrong."

"Eden, you're killing me. You're lying here in nothing but my shirt telling me things I wanted to hear for a very long time, but if I'm going to be honest, I need this to stop. I have to leave you in New York. I need to be able to walk away and go back to my life."

She cupped his face and pressed her warm, soft lips against his cheek. "Make love to me, Ajax. One more time."

CHAPTER 8

EDEN COULDN'T BELIEVE what she just said, but she wanted Jax to make love to her even if it would be the very last time. Because it would be the last time. She could take the memory with her anywhere she ended up after the story hit. Remembering the way he would feel on top of her and inside her would be the thing to help her survive.

"I can't." He slipped from the bed and moved around the small space. Even in the dark, she could make out the movement of him pulling his shirt over his head.

"Why not?"

He stopped with his foot half-way in his boot. "Are you shitting me?"

"Tell me why not." She climbed out of the bed and faced him.

"Lady, what do you take me for?"

"I don't understand. You're mad because I want to make love with you?"

"Yes, damn it. You can't just show up out of the blue needing my help and then ask me to have sex with you to ease your guilt over the way you dumped me. That's on you. If we were ever to make love again, it would be because you wanted to be with me for good. I don't want to fuck you. I want to make you mine."

Could they possibly have a second chance? But she'd be dragging him into her mess more than she already had. If she said she wanted to be his, he'd demand she give up the story, and she couldn't do that. This was her chance to make a name for herself outside of her family. After the story hit and after she got the accolades she needed then she might be able to do something else. Something less risky.

She reached for her yoga pants and shoved her legs in. "I need to go for a walk. You can have the bed."

"I don't want you going out there alone."

"No one is on this train that knows who we are." The walls were closing in on her. She'd just spilled her soul out to him, and he didn't want her. She had to get away.

"I can't take that chance. If you want space, I'll go for the walk. You stay here with the door locked."

"This room is too small. I can't stand it. I want out."

"When will you stop running away?"

His words were like a slap across her face. "What do you want from me? I ask you to make love to me and you reject me. Then when I want to go so I can hide from my embarrassment, you tell me no. You can't have it both ways."

"I need to keep you safe. That's all I ever wanted to do, but you wouldn't let me. You pushed me away time and time again trying to do everything yourself. You had nothing to prove to me. I loved you for who you were. I never cared about your family or your place in it. I wanted us to have our own family so we could make our own choices and live our lives our own way."

The pain etched in his words cut her in half.

"I'm sorry. I'm so terribly sorry for what I did." The tears spilled down her cheeks. "I made the worst mistake of my life by leaving you when you needed me. I crumbled. I'm not strong like you. Always doing the right thing. Living by an honor code impossible for me to match. Always thinking of everything. You would have been the perfect father, and I was afraid I'd be exactly like my mother."

She choked on the tears. Her throat burned. All the things they never said to each other she was trying to say now. She had only heard his desire to have a large family regardless of what she wanted. But once again, he'd thought it all out. She should have realized when she had the chance.

"You are strong." He cupped her face in his hands and pressed his lips to hers.

Her brain needed a second to catch up. He was kissing her and he tasted minty and clean. She snaked her arms around his neck and tangled her fingers in his hair. Every nerve ending in her body caught fire. He parted her lips with his tongue and she remembered all the times he kissed her. And every time was better than the last.

She wanted to get closer to him and pressed her body against his. The darkness made her bold. Tonight would be the only time, and she wanted every second to be perfect.

Every part of her body begged for him to touch her more. She ran her hands under his shirt to feel the flex of his muscles under her fingers. He groaned and pushed his hands under the sweatshirt to find what had been his once.

Their hands searched and moved with urgency. She wanted to slow down and make it last, but she burned hotter for him. She couldn't wait and tugged him over to the bed and helped him out of his clothes. His body was long and toned. She drank in the sight of him as he moved over her. He always kept her safe and in his arms was the only place she wanted to be.

He yanked his sweatshirt off of her. "I want to turn on the light so I can see you."

"Don't get up from this bed. I don't want to let you go." She didn't want to risk anything that could end their connection.

His lips were on her neck leaving a hot trail down to her breasts. She arched up into him. His rough fingers stroked her stomach and ignited her flesh.

"Jax, touch me." She pushed his hand farther down her belly.

"I want to make this last, babe."

He must be thinking this would be their only time too. He would leave her in New York and walk away. She deserved that. Still, the tears threatened to come. She didn't want to cry now.

She reached for him and wrapped her hand around his thick desire. He growled, and she tried not to giggle with pride. The power to make him feel good only turned her want for him up higher. "I want you to feel the way you make me feel," she said.

He dragged his hand down her side and over her thigh. He sought out the center of her heat, and she sighed. Her hips moved to the rhythm he set.

She kissed him again and forgot about everything else except the pressure of his touch on her most sensitive spot.

He moved on top of her and laced his fingers through hers. His erection pressed against her. "You ready?" he whispered.

"Still giving a lady the warning?" How many times had he said that to her right before?

"Only to you, babe."

Her breath stalled thinking she had been special to him. Even if he'd had other women, he hadn't forgotten what they shared.

"Oh, shit. Do we need a condom? I didn't think about it until now." He started to slide away. "I might have one in my wallet."

She gripped his shoulders. "I have it under control."

"You sure?"

"Absolutely. Finish making love to me."

He entered her and took her soaring. The train blew its whistle as it whizzed through another town. They rocked together with the sway of the big, silver engine.

She wrapped her legs around his waist wanting to feel all of him. This was exactly how she wanted their last time together to be. With love. And no regrets. She bit her lip to keep the quivering from starting. He couldn't know she was seconds away from crying. She loved him as vast as the Montana sky. It would always be him.

He waited for her to call out his name and then met her on the other side of the sweet explosion. Their chests heaved, and her skin was damp. She kept her arms around him as if he were a life-line.

She had hidden one thing.

She had nothing under control.

Least of all the birth control.

CHAPTER 9

Jax reached for Eden, but her side of the bed was empty. He propped up on an elbow. The room was still dark. He must've fallen asleep, but it couldn't have been for long.

"Babe?"

He pushed off the bed and took the two steps through the cabin. Not there. Where the hell did she go?

He flipped on a light to check for a note. Nothing. Did she regret what happened? But she seemed so sure she wanted him. He would never have made love to her if he doubted her sincerity for even a second. He did get caught up in the things she said, though. He may have let his heart take the lead when he should have stayed more focused, but he had wanted her so much. He thought he could handle one more time with her and believed she could too. They would still part ways in New York, but tonight would keep him going because he doubted he'd ever feel for another woman the love he felt for Eden. She had reached inside his soul and taken hold.

He shoved his legs into his jeans and threw on his shirt. He grabbed his gun just in case and went out into the hall. The train was quiet at this hour. He passed through the empty dining car and into the lounge.

Eden sat alone in a club chair with a puffy back and faced the window. The night stared back at her broken by the occasional street light off in the distance. She cradled a whiskey glass in her hands. No one manned the bar.

He settled into the chair beside her. "Hey."

She turned and pressed her lips together. "Did I wake you when I left? I'm sorry."

"You okay?" He wanted to reach for her but hesitated. In the bright light of the train car, everything that had just happened seemed to be a smoke-filled dream.

"Sure."

"Did you steal that drink?" He pushed a lightness into his voice.

"I'll pay them for it in the morning. I needed something, and no one is here." She turned back to the window.

"It wasn't locked up?"

She shrugged.

"Christ, Eden, you can't steal." How upset was she?

"Jax, shut up, please. My world is hanging by a thread at the moment. I am sitting on the biggest thing in my career that will also destroy me, my house was torched, and I just made love to the only man I ever cared about after seven years. I needed a fucking drink."

He took her hand. "Are you sorry about earlier?"

She met his gaze with her tear-filled one. "Not one second. Don't you even think it."

He knelt down in front of her. "Don't turn that story in. Come with me to the parole hearing instead. Then we'll go back to Montana together."

She opened her mouth. The door at the end of the car slid open. The trench coat guy came in holding a book and wearing his robe and pajamas.

"Oh, excuse me. I didn't think anyone would be up at this hour. I hope I didn't interrupt anything."

Jax slid back into the chair next to Eden. "Not at all."

She reached over and took his hand. Relief washed over him. Maybe she wouldn't push him away this time.

"Where did you get that drink? I sure could use one. I'm Marty, by the way. I should have introduced myself this afternoon." Marty turned in circles, looking for the source of Eden's inebriant.

"Eden and Jax." Jax stuck out his hand.

Eden grabbed the bottle and two glasses. "Don't tell anyone. I made myself at home, but I plan on paying for this in the morning."

"How did you get that bottle?" Marty said.

"I have some skills." She poured for Marty and him.

"Your wife is a cat burglar." Marty laughed and clanked his glass against Eden's.

"Let's say I can find things when I need to."

"What do you do, Jax?" Marty settled into the chair opposite Eden and sipped his drink.

"I'm in security. What about you? You said you were taking the train for business. Why not fly?"

Marty leaned forward. "I hate flying. Scares the life out of me. There's something special about a train. Forces you to slow down, take in the scenery. Remember why we're on this planet in the first place." He guzzled half the glass.

"That's pretty profound for a train ride," Eden said.

Marty pointed at her with his glass. "You know, you look familiar. Are you from Chicago?"

"No."

He needed to steer old Marty away from pinning Eden because it was just a matter of time. "Marty, are you married?"

"Me? Divorced. Twice. You two newlyweds don't want to hear what I think about marriage. Let's drink to more success for you than I had." He poured another round.

"I'm pretty sure I've seen you somewhere before. Are you an actress?" Marty's laugh took a louder turn.

Great. The guy was getting drunk. "Eden, we should get back to the cabin." He stood and hoped Eden would follow.

"Why the hurry?" Marty said.

"It's late. We should get back." Eden draped her hand on his arm. He pulled her close.

"You didn't answer my question." Marty looked over his shoulder as if someone else could hear him. "You are an actress. You're that lady in that movie where your husband is the killer, right?"

"I'm sorry. That's not me. Good night, Marty. Those drinks are on me, okay?"

Marty stood on wobbly legs. "It's rude to drink and run, Eden." He tipped his head back and downed the rest. "You know, I think I do know you. Your uncle is up for the Supreme Court seat. I saw you being interviewed. You're a reporter too. You have the same eyes.

"He's a good man, your uncle. He's going to do great things on that court. Don't you think? That woman has no right to take away his chance at success. She probably went to bed with him willingly, and now she's changing her story for the fifteen minutes of fame. I hate women who do that." Marty stepped closer. "Don't you agree that people making up stories should be stopped?"

Jax put himself between Eden and Marty. "Back up, pal. You may have had too much to drink."

"I'm fine. You agree with me, don't you, Eden?" He poured another drink.

"Actually—"

Jax gripped her shoulder. "Babe, let's go." He hoped she wouldn't pick now to defend her case. Even without the proof, this was the kind of thing that would get her going. He loved how feisty she could be, but now wasn't the time.

"Hang on a second. Marty, that woman said she was forced, and I believe her. Why would anyone say they were raped when they weren't? And why bring it up now? She doesn't have anything to gain by coming forward on a lie. I hate it when men assume they have the right to shove their dicks where they aren't wanted."

"Okay, let's go." He tugged her away before she ended up in a fist-fight.

"You should watch what you say, Eden." Marty called after them.

Jax herded Eden through the dining car and back to their sleeper car. "Have you lost your mind?" He locked the door and wiped his face with his hand.

She paced the tiny space. "Can you believe that guy?

What nerve. I'm definitely running with that story just to shut men like him up. I wanted to hit him with that whiskey bottle."

"Babe, you need to stay hidden until we get to New York. You can't go shooting your mouth off to some ignorant guy you don't know."

"I couldn't let him get away with what he said, Jax. That's wrong."

"He could be a plant for Christ's sake. Don't you get it?" He needed to get through to her, or she'd end up dead.

She flinched. "A plant? Really? How?"

"I don't know how. I do know that when someone is determined to do something, especially if that someone is about to be appointed to the Supreme Court, he's going to do whatever it takes to make that happen. Your uncle isn't going to stop until you're stopped. Am I making myself clear yet?"

She stared at him.

"Eden? Why did you go into that lounge car anyway? What were you running from?"

"You."

THE SKY FADED from black and spilled muted grays into the cabin. Dawn was waking up. The train would be in Saint Paul as soon as the sun climbed out of bed and over the mountains. Eden waited for Jax to say something, but he stood there with his mouth hanging open.

"Are you afraid of me?" He narrowed his eyes.

"I'm afraid of how I feel around you." Afraid they may

have made a baby. He would be angry when he found out she lied. She wasn't trying to trick him. She just didn't want the moment to end.

Jax's phone sang out and broke the tension. "It's Lincoln. I need to get this. What's up?" he said into the phone.

She busied herself with brushing her teeth and pulling her hair back into a ponytail trying to give him some privacy.

"Are you sure?" Jax said. "No more than an hour. We'll be ready. Thanks. Eden, come out of the bathroom."

She peeked around the wall. "Is it bad news?"

He gifted her his smile. "Pack up. Boomer Rayne will meet us at the next stop and take us to a small airport where we'll be taken to Chicago."

"Is that a friend of yours?"

"He's with the Brotherhood too. Great guy. Former SEAL. A dad. You'll like him."

"I'm going to like him because he's a dad?"

"Did I say something about him being a father?"

"You did."

"I doubt it. Why would I bring that up? Hurry up and pack. We can grab a quick breakfast if you're hungry."

She suspected he brought up the dad thing because deep down he always wanted to be one. He wanted to be a dad just like his. Jax had that perfect family everyone dreamt about. She certainly had because her family was always about winning at all costs. And she never had her mother around. But Mrs. Montero was always there guiding her five children. She cleaned houses for a living while Jax's dad was a cop. Just like Jax.

"Jax, some day you'll be a good dad too." She kept her back to him.

"Kids aren't in the cards for me any longer." He zipped up his duffel.

She grabbed his arm. "Thank you for this trip."

He wrapped his arms around her and pulled her close. She soaked in his smell and leaned against his strong chest. In his arms was the only place she ever wanted to be.

"You don't have to thank me for anything. I always wanted you to be safe and happy, okay?" He kissed the top of her head.

She closed her eyes and took a deep breath. "Is there any chance for us?"

"I wish there were, but we are just too different. You want your career, and I want to protect you from it. I want a big family with lots of kids and you don't. It's okay, Eden. Right love, wrong time kind of thing. It happens. You'll always be special to me and I'll always be here if you need me."

Her heart splintered into a million pieces, but she held onto him. "Why do I have to choose and you don't?"

"The choice was made for me. I can't be a SWAT team member anymore. My job isn't as dangerous any longer. I come home at the end of every day. I can't handle knowing you run around the world investigating stories that might get you killed. I want you sleeping next to me night after night, but I will never ask you to give it up for me. I was wrong about that. I know that now."

Her father's words rang in her head like a gong. Family and love came ahead of everything else. He was the black sheep of the family for that view point. And she'd never listened. She wanted a career and a name of her own. She wanted to prove she could make it on her own. Instead, she betrayed Jax and did it again while they made love last night.

"Thank you for taking me to New York."

"Babe, I'd take you to the end of the world. Let's get something to eat before we pull into St. Paul. And let's try to avoid that creep Marty, okay? I don't want you getting into any more fights." He eased away from her and tossed his duffel over his shoulder.

His mind was made up. She had lost Jax again.

CHAPTER 10

RAIN MET them at the train station in St. Paul. Eden zipped up her jacket as she and Jax waited by the doors to exit. She slipped her hand into his which brought his gaze down to hers. He gifted her with his bright smile.

"Don't be nervous. Boomer will be waiting, and he'll drive us straight to the airport where we'll catch that private plane to Chicago. Then we switch planes to New York. Simple."

"What happens in New York?"

"There will be a car waiting for me at JFK. I'll drive you wherever you need me to. But then I have to hit the road. I need to get to the parole hearing."

"You never told me which case this is. Why are you sitting in on someone's parole? Did you arrest this person?"

He shifted the bag on his shoulder and kept his gaze out the window. "It's an old case. I go for a friend who can't go himself."

She didn't believe him. He never complained about his leg, but sometimes he favored the good one when he thought no one was looking. He hadn't been shot in New York, but that didn't mean the guy who shot him didn't end up doing time there. "Are you making sure the man who shot you stays behind bars?"

He snapped his gaze around.

The door from the lounge car slid open, and Marty weaved out. If the train wasn't swaying so much, she'd swear he was still drunk.

"Well, if it isn't the lovebirds." He tugged on the collar of his trench coat. He held his suitcase in one hand.

"I thought you were getting off in Chicago," Jax said.

"Change of plans. Seems my ticket was only for St. Paul. My assistant can't find her way out of a paper bag. She's my wife's sister. You know how it is with family."

"No, I don't actually," she said.

"Then I guess you're lucky. Do you want to share a cab?"

"I forgot something in our cabin." Jax snapped his fingers. "If you'll excuse us."

Marty blocked their path back into the train cars as the train pulled into the station. They would have to get off, and he'd be right behind them, but Jax faced Marty and eased her behind him so he blocked her. Jax never let go of her hand.

"Step aside, Marty." Jax clenched his jaw and stood toe to toe with the man.

Marty inched back. Jax's broad frame would intimi-date anyone, but when he pulled his shoulders back and glared at whoever he was looking at, even Lucifer would question his motives.

"Can't do that. I'm sorry. You seem like very nice people, but I answer to someone pretty powerful. I need you to get off this train and go with me. If you don't make a fuss, no one will get hurt. We just want the tape. Nothing more." Marty shoved his hand in his pocket. What could only be a gun pushed against the fabric.

She gasped.

Jax's arm shot out, and he clipped Marty in the throat. His eyes bulged, and he reached for his neck. Jax threw a punch and collided with Marty's face. Bones cracked. Blood gushed from Marty's nose.

The train doors opened. Jax grabbed her hand and dragged her onto the platform. He ran without looking back. Other patrons ambled on and off the train lugging bags and blocking the way. Jax pushed and shoved while she did her best to keep up. His leg buckled a little, but he righted himself and never stopped.

The Union Depot waited in front of them with its big columns, large windows, and waiting areas, but Jax ran away from the building.

She wanted to look over her shoulder to see if someone followed them, but she didn't want anything to slow her down. She kept her gaze on Jax's back.

"Fuck, where is he?" Jax stopped in the pickup area and turned in circles. He rubbed the thigh of his bad leg.

"Would we be safer inside?" She wanted him to be okay, and all this running might be bad for him.

"Too many places someone could be waiting." He pulled her behind a parked car and dragged his phone from his pocket. He swiped away at the screen. "Linc, man, he's not here. I just beat the shit out of someone tracking us. I need fucking help. Now."

JAX'S KNUCKLES hurt from pounding Marty. He and Eden had been made and now they had no way out. The train blew its whistle and rolled away. Even the big silver machine was lost to them. Did that fucker get off and follow them? Had someone called the police because a guy in a trench coat lay bleeding on the floor?

"Linc, where is Boomer?" He searched the nearby area, but he didn't recognize anyone. He pulled Eden against him to shield her. He doubted a sniper was on the building, but he learned not to trust anyone.

"I'm tracking his GPS. He should be there. In his truck. Are you sure you don't see him?" Linc clacked his keyboard on the other end of the line.

"He's not here. I need a car. Can you get me one?" His leg ached. He had almost spilled over on the sidewalk when his foot hit the groove in the pavement. That damn wound continued to take away his chance to be there for Eden. He wasn't a man if he couldn't take care of her.

"How did someone know where you were?" Linc said.

"I'm guessing Eden's friend Emma." He stared down at Eden whose eyes had grown to the size of train wheels.

"She did not tell on us." She tilted her pretty chin up.

"Sorry, babe, but you have to consider the possibility." He wanted to kiss her. He would always want to kiss her.

"Inside the station is a Hertz rental booth. I just rented

a car for Stephen Crosby. Please tell me you brought your full wallet."

"What do you think I am?" He'd only forgotten his extra identification once, and Linc would never let him hear the end of it.

"Keep your eyes open. I don't have the layout of the station. Get that car and get the hell out of there. You're going to have to drive to Chicago."

"What?" Had he heard Linc right?

"The train was late. The plane couldn't wait for you. Something more urgent came up. Hank had to let the plane go. If you don't hurry, you won't make the Chicago connection either. If nothing happens, it will take you over six hours to get there, but I'll see what I can do to make the plane stay put."

"We have to make that plane. I need to be in New York." He couldn't miss that hearing. Gregory Wagner could not walk. Ever.

"Watch your back. That's more important. You hear me?"

"Got to go. Thanks, man. I owe you." He ended the call before Lincoln could say something stupid about Jax not owing him anything. He owed Lincoln everything.

"Let's go." He grabbed Eden's hand.

"No."

"Babe, we don't have time for this. I don't know who's watching. We're on our own out here. Please trust me, right now."

"I've done enough. I've ruined everything. I'll go ahead without you. It's not you my uncle wants. Just take a taxi to the airport and go to New York for your hearing. I'll find a way to get there."

"If we hurry, I'll still make the hearing." He wiped a hand over his face. They didn't have time to argue.

This trip weighed on him. He wanted to keep her safe. That had been the only thing he ever wanted. That and to love her. He couldn't allow her to go on alone. Not this woman. Not his woman, even if she'd never be his again. If he drove his ass off, maybe they'd make the next flight unless something more important came up and in his line of work that was always a possibility.

"Jax, I can't hurt you anymore." Tears filled her eyes.

He cupped her face and leaned in close. "Listen to me. You aren't safe out here alone. You need to come with me. I'll take care of everything until you're in New York. And I'll wait there for you. Run with your story and I'll get you to another safe place after that." He would spend the rest of his life keeping her safe if she needed him to.

She gripped his hands. "I can't ask you to do that."

"I made this commitment to you the first time you smiled at me. Stay close." He didn't wait. They had lost precious minutes.

He weaved them around cars and people until they were inside the grand structure with its renovated windows that let in the sun. They found the rental booth and the parking lot with the car.

His phone buzzed in his pocket. "What's up, Linc?"

"Boomer was in an accident. When the train was late, he circled around the city. On the way back, someone T-boned him."

"Not an accident."

"Maybe. Maybe not. Thomas King has a far reach. If someone spilled that Eden was with you, he made the connection to us. They were watching. Or it was random."

"I don't believe in random and neither do you. Is he okay?"

"He's more pissed off than anything. Are you on the road?"

"Pulling onto ninety-four now."

"Call me when you get to Chicago. Good luck."

"Thanks."

They needed it.

CHAPTER 11

"WHERE IN NEW YORK did you hide the tape?" Jax glanced away from the road to meet Eden's gaze.

She couldn't let him miss the parole hearing. He'd sacrificed too much for her already. And she hadn't sacrificed enough. She had walked away from him to make her mark on the world. She thought she needed to matter in some big way.

What mattered was him. Nothing had destroyed her as much as losing the baby, as when that phone call came saying he'd been shot. She had panicked, and her world had turned black. She was nothing without love and family. Her father tried to teach her that. It took this mess to help her see it.

"Eden, you're not listening to me. Where in New York is the tape?"

"Jax, after this story hits, I'm going to quit."

He glanced at her then back to the road. "What are you talking about?"

"After I run with the story about my uncle, I'm going to call it quits."

"Why?"

"Because I don't want to chase stories any longer." And because maybe they had made a baby on the train. She placed a hand on her stomach.

He laughed. "Yeah, right."

"I'm serious. Why don't you believe me?" Anger pushed her spine straighter.

"Since when are you ready to give up your career? You've been chasing the big story since I met you. Once this thing with your uncle hits, every news outlet in the country is going to want you. You won't be able to walk away from that." He changed lanes.

"I want the truth out. The country has a right to know what kind of man he really is, but that's it. I'm tired of being chased and hunted. This isn't exactly a cross-country vacation."

"You've got that right." He changed again. "I could think of a hundred other places I'd rather be at the moment."

"Does that include being somewhere I'm not?"

"Eden, come on. You know how I feel about you. I've been more than honest about that. Could you go easy on me for a change? I have a job to do now and need to stay focused for the sake of our lives."

"Do you want me or not?" She had to ask. Had to know.

His jaw clenched. "I can't believe you're going to do this now." He hit the blinker again.

"Is someone following us?" She turned to try and see out the window.

"Don't look back." He gripped her arm.

"Oh, no. Who is it?" Her heart picked up speed, and her stomach twisted into a ball.

"I don't know, but something is wrong. I can't figure out how they keep getting a gain on us. We haven't left a trail. I'm certain of it. I'm going to take the next exit and see if that Crown Vic follows us off."

She wrung her hands to keep them away from Jax. He needed both hands on the wheel. He stayed in the middle lane tight on the car in front of them. At the last second, he swung the wheel to the left and slid across the lane onto the off-ramp. She gripped the door to keep from falling into his lap even though she wore a seat belt.

"Did they follow us?" She wanted to look.

He checked the rearview mirror. "I don't…shit, there they are. Hang on."

He took the car to a higher speed. She gripped the door again.

"Where are we going?"

"I'm going to back-track north for a while then head east before heading south again where I can pick up thirty-nine. That will take us back to ninety-four."

"How do you know that?"

He smiled. "I know where all the good fishing is."

"I don't know how you can make a joke at a time like this."

"Joking has kept me alive." He winked.

When this was all over, she would tell him the truth about the other night on the train. "Jax, I'm scared."

He took her hand. "I know. Who wouldn't be? We'll make it."

"Do you promise?"

"My word, babe." He slid his hand away and rubbed his leg. He must be hurting. She wanted him to stop and rest.

He took another exit.

"Well? Did the car follow us?" She said a silent prayer they hadn't.

"I can't tell yet. They fell behind a ways back. They must know I'm onto them. I think we need to make a stop at the next town. I'll pull into the police station and call Lincoln again. Maybe they caught my phone signal. Turn it off, please. I should've done that sooner. I'm sorry. I might be fucking this all up."

"Nothing is your fault, Jax. You've been my hero through all of this. We're not going to make the flight in Chicago, are we?"

He ran a hand over his face. "Probably not."

"I'm sorry. I'm the one fucking things up."

"I'm sorry too."

He hit the blinker again and pulled off the main road onto a two-lane road where the sky seemed to open up and the land went on with not much around.

The town sign came into view. Its white clapboard needed a good paint job, but the script could still be made out. *Welcome to Alibi. Pop. 1,002*

"What kind of town name is that?" Where the hell were they now?

"The kind where someone with troubles needs to hide. But even trouble has one law man. I just need to find him."

"Did the car follow us?"

He checked the mirror again. "Looks like we're good for now. But that probably means they'll wait for us to come back on the interstate. We might need backup to get out of here unless I can figure out the back roads."

"If we're safe for a little while, can I stretch my legs? I hate being in a car for so long. I could also use a bathroom break." She knew he would pull over for her, but never for himself.

Having him help her and be by her side made the heat spread over skin. He kept her safe. But she owed him his freedom. This could get him killed. She needed to find a way to leave him behind and get to New York. It might make sense to wait until they were at least on a major highway. She would ask him again to pull into a rest stop and then she'd ditch him. She'd be able to hide in a large crowd and find a bus.

He pulled into a parking lot. The squat metal building with dirty windows looked as if it had seen better days. The shrubbery was sparse and mangy. The lot was mostly dirt that kicked up as they drove across it. The sign above the door read *Joe Knows Eats*. At the end of the parking lot was a small gas station with one pump.

"How's this for now?" Jax put the car in park. "We're going to need to get gas."

"Do you think it's safe?" Only one other car filled a spot.

"Everybody is probably at work. You're just not used to a town this small." He grabbed the keys and slid from the car.

At least he had a gun. She should be thankful for that

much. She followed him out of the car. The sun warmed her chilled skin. "I thought you wanted to find a police station?"

"We will, but this came up first, and you said you needed the bathroom. Let's go inside and check the place out. Are you hungry?"

"Starving." They never ate breakfast.

He held the door open for her. The inside of Joe's smelled of greasy bacon. The linoleum floor was marked from years of footsteps dragged over it. The long counter was adorned by silver stools topped with broken and cracked wine-red Naugahyde. A man with dirty jeans huddled over a bowl and shoveled a spoon in his mouth. He had a book opened beside him on the counter. He raised his gaze toward them, gave a nod, then went back to his business. The booths were empty, but each had a small juke box attached to the wall under the windows.

"You lost?" A short red-head with eyes painted bright blue and lips bubblegum pink sashayed to the hostess stand. Her name tag read Sissy.

"No, ma'am. My wife and I are looking for a good place for lunch."

"You're lost. Joe, we've got visitors. Follow me." She grabbed two plastic menus and continued her sashay down the aisle of booths to the last one.

Jax took the far side facing the door.

The guy at the counter ignored Sissy. Joe must be in the kitchen. Or Sissy was talking to a ghost. This place brought out Eden's imagination which lately had turned to killers around every corner.

"What can I get you to drink?" Sissy fluffed her hair.

"Two coffees," Jax said.

"I'll be back to take your order." And she sashayed away.

She scanned the menu, but she wasn't as hungry as she thought. She stole a peek of Jax over the top of her menu. His brows furrowed as he read the food selections. "It's just breakfast. It's not a big decision."

He glanced at her. "What did you say? Hey, babe, they have eggs benedict." He went back to reading.

Her blood warmed like thick caramel. She loved everything about him. And she loved him enough to save him from her.

"I'll be right back. I'm going to the ladies' room." She slid out of the booth.

"What do you want to eat? I'll order it for you."

She wanted to memorize every detail about him. The shine in his black hair. The way the lines around his eyes crinkled when he smiled. The way he held her in his arms after they made love. She pressed a soft kiss to his lips. "Thank you for taking care of everything."

"I'm just ordering some food, babe. Though I am pretty good at that."

"I'll have whatever you're having."

She turned and walked away.

CHAPTER 12

JAX WANTED to ditch the car they were driving because whoever was on their tail knew what it looked like. Problem was, he had no way to get another vehicle without stealing one. He could hot wire a car before everything was run by computer, but even if they stumbled upon an old enough model, he wasn't in the business of committing crimes. One criminal in the Montero family was enough.

They were never going to get to Chicago in time to catch the plane waiting for them. Part of what kept their identity hidden was not having a large plane sitting around waiting for no one. After enough time, the pilot would be instructed to take flight. Another plane wouldn't be available for at least twenty-four hours without causing suspicions.

He checked his watch. Eden hadn't returned from the bathroom. He hoped she was okay. Sissy dropped their plates on the table.

"You need anything else?" She fluffed her hair again.

"I think we're good. Thanks."

"Big storm coming in tonight. Are you just passing through?" She craned her neck to look at the sky.

"I think so."

"No one stays in Alibi, but if you don't get out before the weather turns, we have a nice B&B at the end of Main. Holler if you need something."

He needed Eden to come back from the bathroom. The man at the counter pushed his bowl away and pulled the book closer. Sissy passed him on her way behind the counter and patted him on the shoulder. He smiled with thin lips and went back to reading. Seemed harmless enough.

The door swung open and two men came in on the damp air. One guy was tall with a beard and broad set of shoulders. The other was cocaine-addicted thin with long hair and a leather jacket hanging off him. The bearded guy met his gaze and held it for a minute.

Jax reached for his gun and flipped open the holster. He gave the bearded guy the slightest of nods. Where was Eden?

The men took seats at the counter. The guy with the book gave the newcomers a once-over and shut his book. "Sissy, you have any of that cherry pie for me?"

"Keith, you want pie this early in the day? What's the occasion?"

"Can't a man feel like cherry pie with lunch? You're starting to sound like my ex-wife. You fellas should try this. Sissy makes it herself." Keith held up the fork Sissy gave him with the pie.

Jax eased his wallet out of his pocket but kept his gaze on the patrons. He threw thirty bucks on the table. That should cover whatever the bill was.

He would count to ten and if Eden wasn't out of the bathroom he was going in. He didn't like the looks of these two or the way the bearded one kept looking over his shoulder in Jax's direction. He and Eden needed to get on the road and put Alibi and Wisconsin in their rearview mirror.

One...two...

EDEN'S HANDS SHOOK. She wanted to go back out into the diner and sit opposite Jax while he ate and talked to her about anything. She also wanted to climb out the bath-room window and make a run for it. She could make it back to the highway, hitch a ride, and leave Jax alone. What she should have done all along. She never should have dragged him into her messes.

What if he got hurt again? How would she live with herself? If she didn't go back out soon, he'd probably come looking for her. She needed to decide.

The bathroom had a window with a side view of the parking lot. She had been at the window when the Crown Vic pulled into the lot and parked. She was pretty sure that was what Jax said the ones following them were driving. If her mind had been paying attention, she would remember that very important detail. She wasn't much of an investigative reporter, was she?

She said a silent apology to Jax and climbed onto the sink for the second time in ten minutes.

The skies opened up, and rain poured down. The wind picked up and shoved the rain drops on their side. She'd be soaked in a second, and she had left her jacket at the booth.

Voices carried from inside the diner and hit the door. She craned her neck to hear better. Was that Jax yelling? She jumped down and ran out into the diner.

And straight into Jax pointing a gun at two men.

CHAPTER 13

"I DON'T WANT ANY TROUBLE." Jax pointed his Glock at the head of the bearded guy.

Bearded Guy kept his hands in the air, but the scowl on his face said it all. The anorexic one stood behind his friend for coverage. Coward.

Keith had backed away from the counter with his hands raised. "Son, you might want to put that gun down."

"I've got no beef with you, sir."

Sissy dropped down behind the counter. She'd be safe there. He saw no sign of Joe.

Eden came out of the bathroom and stopped short. Her face drained of its color.

"Babe, stand behind me. Now." He didn't do more than glance at her. He needed eyes on the bearded guy.

She sidled up to him. The pressure of her body against his made him want to sigh with relief. Instead, he said, "stay close."

He led her along the booths and kept his gun aimed

right at Bearded Guy. "Open the door. I'm going to follow you out." He hoped Eden would do as he told her.

The door opened, and the wind shoved the rain inside. He backed out and let the door close after him. He turned for the car and his heart nearly stopped.

Someone slashed all four tires.

"We need to make a run for it." He grabbed her hand and took off. He had been right about those guys. If he had hesitated, everyone in the diner would be dead now.

"Our bags." She stumbled behind him but managed to keep up.

"Forget them. We need to hide."

But where do you hide in a town the size of Alibi? Everyone knew everyone else. The town gossips would chew on this before he and Eden hit the street. They couldn't go back to the highway without being spotted. They'd have to wait until the sun set if they were going to have a chance of walking out of this town. They might get lucky if Alibi had a car dealership, but he couldn't trust anyone just yet. He needed backup. But first, a dry place to come up with a plan.

The rain pummeled them. He headed to where some traffic appeared to be. Better to stay visible. Bearded Guy wasn't likely to shoot them in broad daylight on the sidewalk. Too many questions. Which was why he had to pull his gun first.

The road widened, and stores filled both sides. Some had balconies, while others had awnings, but none looked the same. Some were wood and others white clapboard as if someone had dropped them, without thought as to their design, straight onto the road.

The street was empty, probably because of the rain. A few cars were parked at an angle in front of the stores. His clothes stuck to his skin. He kept his head down as they passed the gourmet popcorn store, a deli, and a photography shop.

"Jax, where are we going?"

"There's supposed to be a bed and breakfast at the end of the street." He sure as hell hoped so.

"We're spending the night? I thought we had to get out of here?"

"I need to figure out our next move. I can't do that in one of these shops."

Main Street intersected with Joiner Lane. The shops were behind them and houses pocked with age in front of them. His heart sunk. Had he misunderstood Sissy?

"Right there." Eden pointed to the Victorian-style house blocked slightly by the post office and the large oak tree.

He grabbed her and kissed her hard on the lips. Every nerve in his body took notice. "Let's go."

They hurried up the front walk and took the steps two at a time. He shoved open the front door with a long pane of etched glass, and they stepped back in time.

The main entrance was wide with additional rooms connected on all sides by archways. The ceiling was decorated with crown molding in symmetrical shapes. The wide-planked wood floors were covered with oriental rugs in navy and red. A grandfather clock kept time beside the staircase. The place smelled like lemon and baked bread. Other than the smells, this place was the opposite kind of house he grew up in.

"We're dripping on the floors," Eden whispered.

"Welcome to the Green Mountain Bed and Breakfast. Oh, my. You're soaked."

A tall, thin woman with frizzy, white hair stopped half way into the foyer. She wore blue corduroys and sensible gray shoes that matched the gray wool scarf around her neck, but her eyes were warm.

"Let me get you a towel. Hang tight." She disappeared through one of the arch ways and returned as quickly. "I'm Lolli Fitch. I'm the owner. I'll be right back. Oh, dear. You poor things."

"Jax, what are we doing? This isn't going to cause suspicions? You just pulled a gun on two guys a block away."

He leaned down and whispered in her ear. "You need to trust me. We have no way out of this town by ourselves. Just follow my lead."

Lolli returned with two fluffy white towels. "Dry off. You must be freezing. Where did you come from?"

"Up the street." He pushed a smile on his face and hoped Ms. Fitch would know they meant no harm.

"Are you lost? Because you don't have reservations."

The woman was smart to ask so many questions of dripping wet strangers in her lobby. He glanced at Eden who dried her hair with the towel and turned his glance back at Lolli. "We are. And we're having some car troubles. I need to call my brother to come and get us, but he won't be able to get here until tomorrow. He's in another state. Do you have a room we could use for the night?"

"And a dryer." Eden held her wet shirt away from her

skin. Images of what was under that shirt popped into his mind.

"We have a garage in town that can fix your car. Buford can fix anything. I can call him to come and get your car. Where'd you break down?"

"Up on the highway. We walked into town. My brother is a mechanic. He'll get us up and running in no time. He's the only one I trust with my cars." Hopefully, she'd believe the lie before someone told her about the man who pulled a gun in the diner. A man with a woman that matched their description. It was a stretch, but sometimes truth was stranger than fiction. He'd seen enough of that in his life.

Lolli waved her hand. "Oh, you're one of those men, aren't you? I completely understand. My Stan was that way too. He loved his Porsche. Candy-apple red. No one could touch it but him. Did all the work on it himself. Pity I sold it when he passed. But frankly, I hated that thing. She was his mistress." Lolli laughed, and her crystal-blue eyes lit up.

"I've rambled enough and you must be cold. Let's get you in a room." She grabbed a key from the rack behind her. "There are robes in the closet. Put those on and give me your clothes. I will dry them for you. Snacks are at three, but I can bring you up some tea or coffee now and cookies. I just baked a whole batch."

She led them up the staircase. The runner muffled the sound of their footsteps. He'd never be able to hear if someone snuck up to the second floor. "Does the room face the street?"

"Oh, no. I gave you the honeymoon suite. It faces the

garden and you can see the lake in the distance. It's pretty on a sunny day. The spring blooms are coming in."

She unlocked the door and stepped inside.

"This is very elegant," Eden said.

Large windows they would need to stay away from, but plenty big to climb out of if they required a way to escape. The bed was also big and if this had been a vacation, he would have liked to keep Eden under the covers for several days. He looked out. The first floor roof slanted below one of the windows. They might be able to hang from that and jump without causing too much trouble. Christ, he hoped Lincoln could get there fast.

"Can I see your identification? Goodness, I didn't even ask for your names." Lolli's face bloomed red.

"We're Steve and Eden Crosby." He dug his wallet out of his pocket and grabbed the alternate ID. He also handed her a credit card which would alert Lincoln of their whereabouts.

"Well, it's very nice to meet you. I'll run this through just for incidentals. You can pay when you check out. Why don't you go ahead and change? I'll wait in the hallway for your clothes." She closed the door behind her.

Eden grabbed the robes from the closet and stripped out of her wet clothes. His breath caught. Her tight, creamy skin glistened. He wanted to run his tongue over her belly and down between her legs. His jeans pulled tight over his dick. He wiped a hand over his face.

"Jax, why are you standing there? Give me your clothes. Lolli is waiting." Eden tied the belt around her waist and held out her hand.

"I need to make a call first." If he took off his pants now, she'd know exactly what had him frozen in place.

She scowled. He pulled his shirt over his head, handed it to her, and turned on his phone to dial Lincoln.

"Ajax, don't be rude. That nice woman is helping us." She shook her hand.

"Just a second." He grabbed the robe and stepped into the bathroom.

"Smith." Linc's voice came over the line.

"Hang on a minute, Linc." He removed his gun and peeled off his jeans. His skin was wet, and his leg hurt. He put on the robe before opening the door.

Red blotches covered Eden's neck and she clenched her jaw. His blood warmed as she stood there wrapped in that cute robe and mad as hell at him. She yanked the jeans out of his hand and went out into the hall.

"Linc, I need backup." He told his friend what had happened. "We're trapped."

"I have my go-bag in my hand. If this storm doesn't stop me, I'll be wheels up in twenty minutes. It's about an hour and half flight and then the drive. Maybe three hours. Can you stay hidden until I get there? I might be able to find someone closer to you if you can't wait for me."

"I'll manage. You're the best at what we do. And the only one I can impose on. I want my job after this is over."

Linc laughed. "Looks like both of our love lives got in the way of the job."

"Yeah, at least you got the girl in the end." He slid his gun into the pocket of his robe.

"No patching things up?"

"Afraid not."

"I'm in the truck now. Stay safe, bro. I'll let you know when I take off."

"Thanks, Linc, I–"

"You don't owe me shit." Linc ended the call.

Jax hung his head. He needed a drink.

The door opened, and Eden slipped inside. "Lolli said she'd come up in about ten minutes with tea and our clothes. Looks like we sit and wait."

"We'll be out of here by nightfall. If we drive all night, you can be in New York sometime tomorrow."

"How's your leg?"

"Excuse me?"

"You keep rubbing your leg above your knee. Is the damp weather bothering you?"

"I'm fine." His leg had been aching since the train. He hated the reminder of what his life was like before the accident, but he liked that she noticed.

He needed to get to that parole hearing to keep that bastard in jail. The bastard's prison sentence was the only saving grace for what he lost.

"It's okay if you're not fine. Is there something I can do for you?"

"Eden, please drop it." Because it wasn't worth talking about. He couldn't make the injury go away. He couldn't have his life the way it was before the injury. He had tried to move forward, but he was stuck.

"You don't have to continue to push me away. It might help to talk about what happened to you."

Not to her.

A knock on the door saved him. He motioned for Eden to move away. "Who's there?"

"Steve, it's just Lolli. Can you see me through the peep hole?"

He checked. Lolli stood back and waved her arms as if she were controlling traffic. He slid his hand into his pocket and opened the door a few inches.

Lolli rolled in a cart carrying tea in a white pot with pink flowers all over it, two mugs, and a plate of cookies. The tea pot was something his mother would serve her guests with. On the bottom shelf, their clothes were folded. He wanted to get out of this stupid robe and look like a man again.

"I'm so grateful for the dumbwaiter. I don't know what we'd do if we had to carry room service up the steps." She poured the tea. "I'm afraid the sheriff is downstairs. He says he needs to speak to you about your car. He found it abandoned." She handed him back his card and ID.

"How did he know we were here?" Eden said.

"Keith has been the sheriff for a very long time. Everyone likes and respects him. Crime is at an all-time low. Should I tell him you'll be right down? Bring your tea, Steve."

"We'll be right there. Thank you." He closed the door after Lolli and checked the peep hole.

She wasn't standing in his line of vision. He waited for what should be enough time for her to get downstairs. "Hurry up and get dressed."

"What do we do? Is it one of the guys you held the gun on?"

"I think it was the other man. Sissy had called him

Keith. They might be together. The sheriff could be corrupt. We can't take any chances. We'll have to make a run for it and hope we can hide until Linc gets here."

"Jax, it's still pouring. We don't even have jackets since we had to leave the diner without them. This is ridiculous. I'll call my uncle and tell him I won't use the tape. I can wait to run with the story. He'll think I gave up, and he won. He won't suspect me to run with the story later."

"He won't believe you." He shoved his feet in his boots.

"Why not? I've never lied to him before." She dropped the robe and pulled her shirt over her head.

He tried not to stare.

"It doesn't matter that you're honest. He isn't. And you have the evidence to prove it. He will want that tape and you out of the picture. You're a liability, babe, and I won't let him touch you. Let's get that tape and get you somewhere safe." He holstered his gun and grabbed a cup of tea.

"You want something to drink right now?"

"I might need a distraction."

CHAPTER 14

EDEN HELD on to the back of Jax's shirt to keep her hands from shaking. They were walking to their deaths. If Jax was afraid, he didn't show it. He never did. That was something else she loved about him. He stared fear in the face and gave it the middle finger.

Except when he'd been shot. The fear had changed him that night. He held her hand and cried. She didn't know how to handle her big, strong, alpha male crying. She was a terrible person. She needed to make this whole fiasco right somehow. For his sake.

The grungy man from the diner waited by the front door. Lolli was nowhere in sight. Eden's heart pounded on her ribs wanting to get out as much as she did. She took a deep breath and prayed.

"Mr. Crosby, I'm Sheriff Lor. I'm sorry about your car."

She stopped behind Jax. Would she be able to make a run for it again? Would they get away this time?

"Thank you," Jax said.

"I took the liberty of having Buford tow it to his garage. The tires will be fixed free of charge. Alibi didn't give you folks a warm welcome."

"That's not necessary, sir."

"I believe it is. I don't like trouble in my town, and you had yourself a handful."

She couldn't figure out what this guy was getting at. Jax seemed to be playing along so she would stand there and wait for the moment when they ran. She kept her hand on his back.

"When will the car be finished?"

"Buford said give him a few hours. He's making you a priority. I'm real sorry about what happened earlier. I suspected those men were up to no good, but you were faster on the draw. You trained or something?"

"I'm not sure what you're getting at." Jax sipped the tea.

"Mr. Crosby, I watched those men drive to the town line myself. Now, normally I get good and mad when someone draws a gun on me while I'm having my lunch, but like I said those men smelled like trouble when they walked in. I'm never wrong about my sense of smell, if you follow me. You and your missus were just fine sitting at Joe's. Since you're strangers, I have to guess you might be in some kind of trouble. But since you have a keen eye and fast arm, I also guess you've handled yourself in that kind of situation before. So I can call it quits for the night and get out of this rain, I ask you, you trained or are you one of those cartel men?"

"Are you familiar with the cartel?" Jax put the tea down.

"I've met a lot of shady people in my day. Now, you and your wife don't make my nose wrinkle up, so I'm guessing you're not one of those drug smuggling fellas. But if you are, I promise you, you won't make it out of Alibi alive. There isn't much I'm afraid of, if you get my drift. My dinner is home waiting for me, so would you mind answering my question without a fuss?"

Jax looked down at her. "It's okay, babe. I promise." He turned back to the sheriff. "I'm former SWAT until I was injured. Now I'm in security."

"Glad you didn't say the cartel. I would hate to mess up Lolli's foyer with your blood. Do you need some help? I can lend my services to you if more trouble is going to roll into my town tonight."

"We don't mean to cause you any problems. We need a few hours, and then we'll be gone. You'll never see us again."

"Lolli, do you have the place closed up tight for the night, darlin'?"

Lolli came out of the kitchen holding a shotgun. "Sure do."

Eden gripped Jax's shirt harder.

"Good night then. Lock the door behind me. Holler if you need anything." Keith turned and went back out into the rain.

"Now, don't be afraid," Lolli said. "You're safe for the night."

"Why are you helping us?" Eden said.

"Because you're good people in trouble. And Alibi is a town made for people who need help. Keith told me about your car and those men. Someone is hunting you. We don't want to know why, and we don't want to get involved, but we want you to be safe. At least while you're here. Now, get some rest. That storm is really kicking in. No one's going in or out of town tonight."

"WILL YOU PLEASE SIT DOWN? Lincoln will be here soon."

Eden paced past the queen-size canopy bed in their room. If they had been on vacation, instead of running for their lives, she might have enjoyed the scalloped wallpaper and the satin comforter. Or the ornate carvings in the bed frame and high-back chairs. Jax had lit a fire, which was nice, but the heat was choking her.

"How can you be so calm?" She tugged at the collar of her shirt.

"Because I'm a good shot." He gifted her his smile.

She heated up more. "You aren't worried? How do we know that sheriff is really a good guy? And what about Lolli with that shotgun? Did you see it? That little lock on the door isn't going to keep anyone out, and I don't care what kind of a shot you are. If she pulls off a round before you do, that shotgun trumps your fancy pistol any time."

He crossed the room and placed his hands on her shoulders. The fire danced in the dark brown color of his eyes. She wanted to fall against him and let him take care of everything.

"Babe, if they wanted us dead, we would be. Keith could have called Lolli and told her we were headed her way. She had our clothes. We were at a disadvantage.

We're okay until Lincoln gets here. Then we'll hit the road and get you to New York."

"That storm isn't going to let Lincoln anywhere near us." She pushed his hands away and went to the window.

The dark night made it impossible to see out. The wind howled on the other side of the glass and the rain banged against the house begging to get in. No one was safe out there.

Jax shoved the dresser in front of the door. "Does that make you feel better?"

"Are you making fun of me?"

The smile tugging his lips made her want to kiss him and smack him at the same time. Everything that had happened in the past few days had all her muscles tied up, and he could stand there making light of a terrible situation. She wanted that gift, but she did not have it.

"I would never make fun of you. I just want to wipe that crease away from your eyebrows. It's going to be okay."

"Nothing is okay. I'm almost sorry I started this whole mess. I thought I was doing a good thing giving my cousin a heads up. I wanted him to have time to clean up any messes he had lying around. I know about an affair he had a few years ago. He doesn't know I know that, but I went digging."

"Of course, you did."

"It's my job. I can't turn it off. You don't turn yours off. You're always eyeing up every room you walk into. You never keep your back to the door."

"Our jobs aren't the same. You expose people's ugliest sides. That's usually a good thing when it's corruption and terrorism. But innocent people usually get dragged into it against their will."

"Innocent people get hurt when you do your job too." Her fists clenched at her sides. A storm brewed inside her like a hurricane rolling off the horizon toward shore. She couldn't push it away or send it back, but she wanted to be mad at someone.

Maybe everything had caught up to her. Every minute of the last seven years.

"Sometimes that's true, but most cops aren't in the business to hurt people. They get into the work to help."

"I help people." She did. Sometimes. She was helping the woman accusing her uncle of raping her. No one believed that woman. The media made a joke out of her by questioning her motives. Her uncle called her names and accused her of being a drunk and a liar.

"Reporters want the story. They don't care how they get it or who gets hurt because of it. It's all about the headline, isn't it? You might be helping this woman with your breaking story, but don't you still want to make a name for yourself? To prove you're more than another King? Would you be this hell-bent on getting the scoop if you were someone else in the same situation?"

He saw right through her, and it tore her heart in half. "Shut up, Jax. Just shut up."

He stepped closer. "Why? Because you don't like what I'm saying? Too bad. You need to hear it. You're going to get killed. And for what? Why not just hand that tape to the authorities and walk away? When is something going to be more important to you than the story?"

"When are you going to accept me for who I am?" The

storm rolled in and crashed against her. Her insides shook. She wanted him to see her for her and not who he wished she would be.

"I do. I don't like your job. That's it."

"No, you want me to be someone I'm not."

"Why are we having this fight, Eden? I don't want to fight with you like it's seven years ago."

"Why can't you love me as I am, Jax? I never quit my job because I felt like you were forcing me to choose between you and it. I never made you choose."

"You left me instead, lady." He turned his back on her.

"Don't turn away from me." She ran over and shoved him. "I want to have this fight."

His eyes grew wide and his jaw ticked. Good.

"Calm down before Lolli comes running."

"You can't hide from me any longer. Here we are stuck in this room until your partner comes. You're going to tell me how you feel."

"You know how I feel. Why do I have to say it again? I loved you. You left me. End of the story."

"That's not it."

"What are you talking about?"

"You're still mad at me. Isn't that what your trip to New York is really about? You're hurt and angry and want to take it out on someone. You're mad at me for leaving you whether you want to admit it or not. You're mad we lost the baby. You're mad as hell at the guy who shot you. You can't let that anger go. You keep it all bottled up inside you and act like you don't give a shit about anything. Big, alpha male has it all under control. Life threw him a curve ball, but it didn't affect him at all. He came back and got on with his life without a blink."

Red blotches dotted his mocha skin, and his brows furrowed. He reached for the spot above his knee, but stopped. "Drop it, Eden. You don't know what you're saying."

"Just say it." Her voice shook the walls.

Veins popped out on his neck. "Woman, you're damn right I'm mad." He growled.

She jumped.

"Everything I ever wanted was snatched away from me in a forty-eight-hour period. Everything I worked my ass off for was gone and there was nothing I could do to get it back. All my plans were over, and I didn't know how to move forward. I was stuck. I wanted to hurt someone. I wanted you to hurt the way I was hurting except you left me and went on with your life like nothing had ever happened."

"That isn't true." She wanted to pound on his chest to make him understand, but she stayed put. "I threw myself into my work because if I stopped for even a second, I couldn't breathe. I lost my baby and I lost you and it was all my fault. You needed me and I failed you because I couldn't handle my own grief. I wanted you to make everything okay like you always did, but you couldn't. You were broken and scared and mad. I panicked."

She was a coward. Always had been. She pushed and browbeat her way through investigations, demanding people take her seriously. She bulldozed her way through every situation because she didn't want anyone to know the truth. She was a fraud. Only Jax saw the real her and asked her to declare the truth, but she wouldn't. Who would she become if she didn't hide behind her family name? Or worse, who would she become if she allowed her identity to be swallowed up by Jax's name and children? Would she turn into her mother and run away? It had been better to leave him before that could happen.

She touched her stomach. She wasn't sure if she could give up now, but this was the closest she'd ever come. She didn't want to hurt him anymore.

"I'm only human, Eden. Even I have my breaking point and that night seven years ago was it." The glare in his eyes turned cold.

He was stashing his emotions away again. His outburst was all he'd give her. She knew him well enough to recognize the retreat.

"Can you forgive me?" She kept her voice low and soft. The storm was out of her now. Only the storm outside continued to pummel the house.

He shoved his hands in his pockets and shrugged. "The past is the past."

"Please, Jax. I need to know you forgive me." Because if they made a baby, they had to get over the past hurts even if he could never really love her again.

"I don't know what you want me to say."

"That you can forgive me. You're still mad. I guess I deserve that, but all that anger is going to eat you alive."

"I'm fine, but thanks for caring."

"If you're fine, don't go to that parole hearing."

He let out a long breath. "Like you're not going to release that story over every social media platform out there. Not to mention, I'm keeping a criminal behind bars. I'm keeping innocent people safe. That's my job."

"You don't have to show up every year. You could even send your request for denial as an email. You have enough clout for that. Any parole board would take your comments to heart no matter how you expressed them." She dropped onto the bench in front of the bed. Her body ached with fatigue.

"I have to be there. I want that guy to look me in the eye and know I'm the one responsible for taking his freedom."

"Like he took yours."

He flinched.

"I'm going to shut my eyes for a while. Let me know when Lincoln gets here."

She climbed under the covers still wearing her clothes. She was too tired to change and couldn't handle undressing with Jax so close. She pulled the blanket up under her neck and closed her eyes.

If only sleep would come. And soon.

CHAPTER 15

JAX NEEDED TO RUN. The poison coursing through his veins burned him from the inside out. He needed to get rid of it and fast. He didn't have a punching bag or a sparring partner. He did have a pain radiating through his bum leg, though.

Eden had the power to incite an anger in him like no one else. And still he loved her. But right now, he needed space. Except he couldn't get any without leaving her alone in the room unprotected.

"Are you asleep?" he whispered.

"Yes."

He smiled in spite of himself. "I'm going to move the dresser and go downstairs. Please lock the door behind me. I'll knock three times when I come back. Don't open the door for anyone else. Even Lolli."

She ignored him.

"Eden?"

"I heard you."

"Will you lock the door?" He shoved the dresser back to its original spot under the gilded mirror.

"I don't want to get out of bed."

"I need you to stay safe."

"Just go, Jax. In fact, when Lincoln gets here, have him take you to New York for your hearing. I'll make my own way there. I'll take the rental car once the tires are fixed."

"Don't do this."

"I don't want to need you anymore."

He didn't want to need her anymore either. But he did. He ran a hand over his face and scratched at his beard. He hadn't bothered to shave since before the train. He was probably looking mangy about now. Not regulation dress code at all.

He closed the door behind him and hesitated. The lock clicked, and he let his shoulders drop. He'd take her to New York if he had to carry her into Linc's car and he might. She was that stubborn.

The storm made it impossible to take a run. Even sitting on the porch was out of the question with the rain coming in on a slant. He checked his phone. Nothing from Lincoln. That wasn't a good sign.

He needed to do something to get Eden's voice out of his head. She was wrong. He had to be at that parole hearing. It was more than anger. It was justice. It was the right thing to do.

The kitchen was closed for the night. The counter was wiped clean. The metal sink gleamed in the small light above it. A pot of white flowers sat in the center of the wood block table.

He opened the fridge hoping Lolli wouldn't mind. Didn't she say they should make themselves at home? Or was that wishful thinking? He grabbed some vegetables from the clear drawer inside the fridge and rummaged through the cabinets for a cutting board.

He cut up the veggies then mixed them in some eggs. He'd pay her for whatever he used. He needed to keep busy. His phone buzzed in his pocket. He wiped his hands on a towel and answered.

"Jax, man. I'm stuck at the airport. The planes are grounded until morning. Can you hold out another six to eight hours?" Linc's voice broke in and out of the connection.

How the hell was he supposed to hang on that long with Eden picking fights with him and threatening to go to New York by herself? "Sure."

"We'll drive straight through to New York. I don't want you trying to get on another plane."

"I don't want you involved that long. Just get me out of this town and I'll get Eden and I where we need to be. I want your ass home with your lady." He dumped the eggs and veggies into a pan.

"The cops are looking for Eden. The person in her house was a source for her newspaper. He'd been missing for a week. It also seems he stopped giving her any information. They had a fight outside her office building. Plenty of people saw it."

"That's motive." He burned his hand on the side of the skillet and shoved it under cold water.

"I'm afraid so."

"She didn't do it."

"I know that. I think you should contact the locals and have her give a statement. She's got an alibi. She was at your place all night."

"Can't do it."

"Jax, man, come on. You know how this works. If she doesn't cooperate, they're going to make it harder on her."

"Her cousin is a cop. We don't know who we can trust. I need someone we know." Maybe he could contact his old partner when he was SWAT. They hadn't spoken in years, all his fault, but they had been like brothers.

"Don't wait on this. Watch your back. I'll see you in the morning."

"Thanks, Linc. I–"

"Shut the fuck up, already." Linc ended the call.

"I owe you," he said into the empty room.

He finished the vegetable omelet and slid it onto a plate. He threw it in the garbage. He wasn't hungry. He returned the kitchen to the way he found it and left a twenty on the counter for the food with a note for Lolli.

"Smells like eggs in here, but the kitchen looks spic and span." Lolli leaned against the doorway in a long, pink robe. Her frizzy hair stuck up in different directions. Her sensible gray shoes were on her feet.

"I made myself at home." He handed her the money and the note.

She handed them back. "I feed my guests. What has you wandering around in the middle of the night?"

"Couldn't sleep."

She moved around the kitchen opening cabinets, pulling out mugs, and firing up the tea kettle.

"I don't drink tea." It tasted as if it was dirty water to him.

"Tea cures a lot of ailments. Do you want to talk about the trouble you and your wife are in?"

"I'd rather not."

She took a seat at the table and patted the spot next to her. "Who's coming for you? It's better if we're all prepared."

"The less you know, the better. Believe me." He sat beside her. He wasn't in any rush to return to Eden. He had nowhere else to go for now. "Why are you helping us?"

"Because we want to keep our little town safe. I know you didn't mean to bring trouble this way. I can see that in your eyes and in the way your wife looks at you. No woman looks at a man the way she looks at you if that man is the trouble."

He was pretty sure Eden looked at him with disgust most of the time. Sure, they had a great night on the train, but she had been scared.

He loved her and wanted to believe she loved him too, but she'd never put him ahead of her work. He didn't know if he could continue to come in second and yet how could he ask her to give up her dreams? What if he did get hurt again on the job and she left him? He'd never survive another heart break like the last one.

The tea kettle whistled interrupting his thoughts. Lolli poured two mugs and put one in front of him. The smell of apple and cinnamon rubbed against his nose.

"Eden isn't your wife, is she?" Lolli held his gaze.

Heat filled his face. "How did you know?"

"By the way you look at her. And neither of you are wearing a wedding ring." She winked.

"What do you mean, by the way I look at her?"

"Young people don't always realize what's right in front of them. You have to get miles away and turn around before you notice what had been standing beside you the whole time. You're wasting a whole lot of time, my boy. Take it from Lolli, time is the one thing we never have enough of. You love her, but you're hesitating about something. Did she hurt you once?"

Lolli's revelation made his skin break out in bumps. He gripped the mug for something to focus on instead of her intense stare. She seemed to look right through him. Kind of like his mother.

"Do you have children?" He wanted to steer the conversation away from him and to find out if all mothers had the power to see inside the minds of people younger than them.

"I have three boys. Rough-houses all of them. They moved away. Alibi's boundaries pushed too hard against men with so much life in them. I bet you'd be the same way here. Go on, now. Drink up. The tea won't hurt you."

There was a time when a small town would have strangled him, but now that he was getting older, he didn't think that would be as true. He envied Linc and his cabin in Winter where he went to get away. Jax wanted something like that. And someone to share it with. He still wanted a house full of kids too.

Out of respect for Lolli and her kindness, he took a

tentative sip of the tea and tried not to spit it back into the mug.

Lolli took his mug away. "Go upstairs and make right whatever is wrong between you and Eden before you have to run again. I'll keep watch from inside. The storm will keep us safe from the outside."

"Thanks."

"Just call me cupid." She laughed and drank her tea.

JAX KNOCKED on the bedroom door three times and waited. Eden didn't answer. He tried again. Nothing. She probably fell into a much-needed deep sleep. He grabbed a credit card from his wallet and jimmied the lock.

The room was dark. Eden's breath came in a slow rhythm. Just as well. He didn't know what he would say to her. She was right. He was angry and not sure how to forgive her. He'd tried through the years, but the hurt ran too deeply.

He kicked off his boots and grabbed a pillow and an extra blanket from the bed. He would sleep on the floor no matter how much he wanted to crawl in bed beside her and tuck her into his arms. The wind continued to howl and shake the glass. A draft wrapped itself around him on the cold, wood floor. He banged the pillow a few times trying to get comfortable.

Sleep pushed at the corner of his thoughts and he was ready to surrender. A warmth brushed up against him, and he stiffened. "Eden?"

"Hi." Her breath was a warm whisper on his neck.

He turned to face her and offered some of the covers. His leg ached in complaint. "It's cold on the floor. What are you doing down here?" His insides warmed, and he didn't feel the cold any longer.

"I couldn't sleep without you." She ran a finger over his jaw.

The electric current of her touch sizzled right to his heart and his groin. If she kept touching him like that, he might take her right on the floor. "I thought you were mad at me."

"Jax," she said his name on a long breath. "I'm sorry. I know I keep saying that, and maybe it doesn't mean anything anymore, but I'm so sorry. I hurt the one person I cared about most in the world. And I might be hurting you now too. I don't know how to move forward. I thought I knew what I wanted, but this time with you has confused all that."

He placed his hand on her low back and pulled her against him. She wrapped her arms around his waist, and he sighed into her. "I don't know what to do either. I thought I had everything under control as long as I stuck to the routine. But you showed up at my door, and now nothing makes sense."

"I don't want this night to end without you knowing how I feel. I may never get the chance again to tell you."

"I'm not allowing you to go to New York by yourself. I won't let you out of my sight, so forget trying to find a moment when you can make a run for it." He inhaled her cinnamon scent.

"I want you to go back to Montana and live your life the way it was meant to be. Without me. I want you to be happy, and I can't do that for you, but I need you to know I love you. I have always loved you. There has never been anyone except you." Her shoulders shook, and his T-shirt dampened with tears.

"Babe, don't cry. I'm the one who should be sorry. I asked you to give up your job because it scared the hell out of me. I hate the idea of you running around the world putting yourself in dangerous situations. How can I keep you safe if you won't stay with me? But I shouldn't have asked you to choose because when I did, you chose the thing that wasn't pressuring you. I'm sorry."

She ran her fingers along his spine setting his skin on fire. "What do we do now?"

"I know what I want to do." He kissed the top of her head. "But I can't again. I can't knowing you want to walk away from me."

Her hands searched under his shirt. Her soft skin drove all his heat south. She had to know how he was affected by this little encounter. There was no space between them and even his jeans couldn't hide everything.

"Eden, say something, because if you keep that up, I'm going to start kissing you."

"What if I didn't walk away?"

He wasn't sure he heard her over the pounding of his heart. "Say that again."

"What if I stayed? No more investigative reporting. I can do something else. Maybe write that book I always talked about."

"Would you be happy in Eagle Rock and not traveling

the world?" He eased the question out a little at a time, afraid to get his hopes up.

"Maybe we could travel a little, you know, together."

"Like vacation?"

She laughed, and the tightness in his chest eased. "Yes, Ajax. A vacation. People do take those."

"I love the sound of my name on your lips." He wanted his name there for the rest of their lives. Calling out to him in bed, from the kitchen when dinner was done, and to have him come running for their children. He removed her hand from his back.

"What's the matter?" She sat up and leaned on an elbow.

He turned to stare at the ceiling. She was telling him what he wanted to hear. Could he possibly ask for more? If she said no, he didn't know how he would handle it.

"Jax? Did I say something wrong?"

Did he push?

"Damn it, Jax. Talk to me. Don't shut me out, please."

He took a deep breath. There would be no going back after this. "What about kids?"

She dropped back down, facing him. "Please look at me."

He couldn't resist her.

She placed a hand on his cheek, and his skin burned right through. "The other night on the train, when I told you the birth control was covered..."

"Yeah?" His heart picked up speed again.

"There was no birth control."

He gripped her hand. "You lied to me?"

"Well, I was going to tell you."

"When?"

"If there was something to tell."

He pushed up from the floor and paced the room. "Let me get this straight. You and I made love, and we could have made a baby, again, and you didn't think it was necessary to mention that to me ahead of time? What were you planning to do, Eden? Get pregnant and run away? I don't understand you." And he didn't understand the pain in his chest. That was a lie. He wanted to avoid the pain in his chest.

She stood in his path. "It's not like that. I knew you wouldn't make love to me if we didn't have any protection, and I needed you. I still need you. If I ended up pregnant, I would have told you."

"What would you have done, called me from the witness protection program? Because that's where you're going to need to be after your story hits."

She gripped his arm, but he tore it away. How could she do this to him? He wanted to punch something. Or shoot something. But he was stuck. In that room, with her.

"Jax, I wasn't trying to hurt you."

"You used me."

She flinched. "I would never do that."

"Really? What was showing up at my doorstep doing? You risked my life without a second thought because you knew I'd help you. And your plan the whole time was to expose your uncle then be on your way without any thought for me. And a bonus for you." He threw his hands in the air. "A baby." He shouted the last words. Probably woke Lolli.

"I was scared. I didn't know where to go. I couldn't trust anyone, but I knew I could trust you. You would never hurt me. You have to know I would never hurt you on purpose."

He leaned in until they were an inch apart. "Thing is, Eden. You have hurt me on purpose. More than once."

CHAPTER 16

EDEN DESERVED WHAT JAX SAID. She wasn't going to argue. She'd left him at the worst possible time of his life. He was never going to forgive her, and she'd gone and made it worse by telling him about having sex without protection.

She let out a long breath. What if they had made a baby? He would do the responsible thing. But he had no space for her in his life any longer.

She stood in her spot in the pretty bedroom as Jax kept his back to her. His muscles flexed under his T-shirt. She wanted to go to him and try to ease the pain, but she was the one causing all his grief. She let him stand there hating her, and she stood there in her constant grief and loved him.

It was a waste to love someone so much. He didn't feel the same way. He didn't look at her as if she were the only person in the room. He saw regret when he looked at her.

He reached into his pocket and pulled out his phone.

"What's up, Linc? You are one amazing bastard, you know that? Okay. In five." Jax shoved his phone back in his pocket and turned to her.

"Lincoln will be here in five minutes."

"How did he manage that?" The storm continued to blast outside. She had hoped for more time to convince Jax she meant what she said. She'd stay for him. She would give up her job, because at the end of her life, she wouldn't care about how many stories she broke. The awards and the accolades would mean nothing with no one to share them with.

"He's that good. Let's go. I want to find Lolli and say goodbye."

She followed him out into the hall and down the stairs. He called for Lolli and the sweet woman with frizzy, white hair came running with her shotgun. Jax laughed.

"Whoa. It's okay, Lolli. My partner is coming to get us. We need to settle our bill." Jax opened his wallet.

Lolli shooed him away. "This stay is on me. I haven't had this much fun in ages. I never get to take my Rita out of the safe. Be careful, you two." She folded them into a big, warm hug and left them in the foyer to wait.

The rain continued to pound the earth, and the wind whistled through the trees. No car came down the road. She wrapped her arms around her middle trying to fend off the cold building in her heart.

"He'll be here soon." Jax checked his phone.

"What's the plan?"

"Linc will drive us all the way to New York."

Great. The three of them in a car for hours. She would never get the chance to talk with Jax about their situation.

He would deliver her to the address she told him, and then he would leave her.

She couldn't let that happen. "Jax, before Lincoln gets here– "

"Eden, don't. I don't want to talk about us anymore. You put the thought of you pregnant in my head, and I need it the fuck out before I lose focus and get us both killed. I can't keep dragging up all our old shit right now. If you make it back to Montana, and only if you're carrying my baby, we can talk then."

"No, damn it. I'm going to talk now. I'm sorry. For everything. For leaving you. For losing our baby. For sleeping with you on the train under false pretenses. But I love you. I need you to understand that. And until we were running for our lives, I didn't know just how much. After my cousin beat me up, I knew the only person who could keep me safe was you. I didn't care if you didn't want me around. In that moment, you were the only person I knew could help me." Her words tumbled over each other covered in tears.

She wiped her snot running nose with the back of her hand.

"I don't know what to say." Jax stared at her.

"Say you'll forgive me."

The rumble of an engine grew as if someone turned the volume knob to the right. She hung her head. Not now. Headlights cut open the dark night as a big vehicle idled out in the street. The headlights flashed a code. Jax shoved open the front door. He took her hand and led her out into the rain.

Without saying a word.

THE RAIN PUMMELED Jax as he ran for the big, black SUV. His clothes were soaked by the time he helped Eden into the back and he ran around to the front. He shut the door and shook his hair as if he were a dog coming in from a run through the river. The windshield wipers swished back and forth in an urgent rhythm fighting to keep up with the water running down it. His heart beat in the same urgent tempo. He tried to ignore it. Eden loved him, might be carrying his child for the second time, and he didn't know if he should completely trust her.

"Man, are you a sight for sore eyes." He shook Linc's hand.

"Thanks for coming, Linc," Eden said.

"Anything for my brother. Now, let's get the hell out of town." Linc turned the vehicle around on the small street.

They left Alibi in the rearview mirror.

"Is anyone behind us?" Jax rubbed his leg. The damp air was killing him.

Linc glanced behind them. "All clear since I left the airport. Every part of communicating has been encrypted. I didn't fly commercial. There's no trace of the flight plan. No one knows I've even left Montana except Serra, Hank, and you two."

"I'm sorry we took you away from her," Eden said.

"That's the job. Sometimes a client needs help in the middle of the night, and you go no questions asked, or a brother needs you and you go. Even faster. The only thing you worry about is the danger so you're prepared."

Linc was talking too much, and he wanted him to shut it. Eden had left him because of his job. And because he pushed her to have a family. Why the sudden change of heart on her part? Okay, it wasn't exactly sudden. They'd been apart seven years. Could she really have missed him?

"What's it...about fourteen hours straight through to New York?" He turned up the heat and pointed the vents right at his legs.

This may be the last day he spends with Eden. He wanted the drive to New York to last so he could smell her cinnamon scent and know she was safe beside him. If she was pregnant, would she really tell him? His chest ached as much as his leg. He didn't want to miss out on his child's life. He'd have to bring up the subject with Linc here. He had no choice.

Linc glanced at him. "If we drive all night we can be there in fourteen hours, but I'm not driving you straight through. I don't want you sitting too long in one vehicle. We can't get a lead on Thomas King, but he's been able to follow you, and I can't figure that out. We need to keep switching you up. I'm taking you to a small airport outside of Chicago. A little town called Chesterton where prop planes fly in and out. The pilot will take you to New York."

"How did you arrange that?"

"Not me. Hank. He called an old military buddy who lives out there and flies. Another flight without a flight plan. But there's one thing you're going to have to do before you can board. There's no other way I can let you take off."

"What's that?" he said.

Eden leaned forward. "I don't like the sound of this."

Linc glanced at him then back at the road. "You're going to have to strip first."

CHAPTER 17

EDEN WAS MORE than happy to strip in front of Jax, but she wasn't going to take her clothes off for Lincoln.

"I don't understand." She positioned herself between the two front seats to see both men. "What's he talking about, Jax?"

"Um, not sure. Lincoln, you know I trust you with my life, but you can't see Eden without clothes on." His jaw twitched, and his brows creased.

Her heart swelled a little. He was jealous. Now, if he wasn't so damn stubborn, maybe they could mend their fences and stay together.

Lincoln gave a full-body laugh. "Lighten up, asswipe. I think Eden was bugged. Probably in her coat. You haven't been followed since the diner where you both left all your belongings. But I can't take the chance your cousin didn't put a bug in your shoe. When we get to the airport, I have a change of clothes, new shoes, and new coats ready for you. I'm going to burn what you're both wearing."

"These are my favorite boots. You can't burn them. Run a wand over them," Jax said.

"You can keep your ugly, beat up boots. But sorry, Eden, nothing of yours stays. Including undergarments." Lincoln met her gaze in the rearview mirror.

She wanted to groan. "I can at least have some privacy while I change, can't I?"

Lincoln laughed again. "It's not like you're in prison. Sit back and enjoy the ride."

Jax glanced at her. "Watching over your shoulder is going to feel like prison. It's not too late to change your mind about all of this."

"It's not too late to change yours either." She leaned back and crossed her arms over her chest.

Lincoln took his gaze off the road and looked at Jax. "Bro, sounds like you're in trouble."

"What else is new?" Jax settled into the seat and kept his head straight ahead.

The rest of the ride passed in silence. She closed her eyes a few times, but sleep never came. She had so much she wanted to say and didn't know where to begin. Or maybe she'd said it all, and the rest was going to be up to Jax. If he wanted her, she would be there and if he didn't then she'd go on. Without him. If she ended up pregnant, she'd have to figure that all out. Could she survive having him in her life if he wasn't anything more than a parenting partner?

The sky spread wide open and started to remove its black cloak for a lighter gray one. Lincoln turned down a long, windy road dotted with the silhouettes of trees. A driveway snaked toward a two-story, clapboard building with the airport's name inscribed across the wall. Behind the clapboard building were two hangars.

Lincoln parked. "Come on inside. I want you to meet Herb. He's your pilot."

They followed Linc into the building. A waiting area with a reception desk occupied the front space. The shiny floors and plastic chairs reminded Eden of a car dealer's show room. Lincoln rang the bell.

A tall man in navy-blue overalls and a red cap came out from the office behind the reception area. He had a pen behind his ear and a warm smile on his round face. His teeth were small, but perfectly in line. His brown eyes shone. Herb had the kind of face that said to trust him.

"Lincoln Smith, I presume?"

The two men shook.

"I am in fact."

"Hank told me what you'd look like. You must be Jax and Eden, the two in trouble. Pleasure to meet you both."

Jax jumped in and pumped the man's hand too. "Thank you, sir. I appreciate the help. We both do." Jax gifted her his smile.

That goofy smile would undo her.

"No trouble at all. When an old buddy calls with a favor, I'm glad to jump in. Makes me feel useful again."

"Do you have the items we requested?" Lincoln said.

"I think you'll be satisfied with what I collected on short notice. I have a cot in the back room. You can change in there. As soon as you're ready, we'll take off. Can have you in New York by this afternoon."

And from there, Jax would take her to the apartment

where the tape was hidden. And leave her for good. She didn't know how to stop that from happening.

"You can go first," Jax said.

She wished he'd come in with her. "Thanks."

The room wasn't much bigger than a closet with shelves stacked with office and bathroom supplies. Sure enough, shoved against the back wall was a small cot neatly made and ready for someone to steal a nap from it. Two piles of clothes lay neatly folded on opposite corners of the cot. A pair of sneakers for each person was underneath and two jackets hung on a peg above the wall. A black one for her and a navy blue one for Jax.

She stripped and piled her clothes on the floor, including her sneakers. Had her cousin John bugged her after he beat her up? She could have slipped unconscious for a while. She wasn't sure.

She shoved her legs into a pair of jeans that dragged on the floor and donned a red shirt that fit well enough. She slipped her feet into the new sneakers and walked out. Lincoln waited right outside the door with his hands outstretched.

"Is this everything?"

"Yes."

"Jax, man, your turn. Hurry up."

"I have the bonfire going in the back like you requested, if you want me to start burning those clothes." Herb smiled with warmth as if nothing they were doing was a surprise. This man must have seen plenty in his life.

Jax snuck past her and shut the door. Five minutes later, he returned in his new clothes that accented his muscular body and still wearing his ugly boots. "Here." He dumped his belongings in Lincoln's arms. "I like those jeans too. I don't know why you don't just run a wand over them."

"Because I forgot to pack one. It's just clothes. We can't take a chance whoever planted the bug was someone else, like your friend on the train. As long as you have your gun, the rest doesn't matter." Lincoln handed the pile to Herb.

Jax patted his side. Relief washed over her. Thank goodness for his gun.

"What about the parole hearing?" Lincoln cut open her sneaker at the seam and peeled back the frame from the bottom.

Jax shrugged and looked over Linc's shoulder watching him dismantle her shoe. "I might still make it."

Lincoln tore away each layer of the bottom of the sneaker and reveal all the support gels and foams put into place for comfortable walking. He ran his fingers along the side of each layer. "Here it is." He crushed the bug under the sole of his boot.

Her stomach hollowed out. "John did that? How?"

"It's not hard. He probably shoved the bug under the removable insole. All your walking would force the bug down farther and embed it in the foam."

"How did he know I'd put those shoes on?"

"I'm afraid this won't be the only bug he left. My guess is these are your favorite sneakers, and he knows that."

"You're right."

"He usually is," Jax said.

"I didn't realize I was unconscious long enough for him to plant bugs." Her skin crawled with the idea of her being incapable of defending herself while he put his hands all over her belongings and possibly her.

"You should be able to get to New York now without any trouble," Lincoln said.

"It's after the story hits that she's going to have trouble," Jax said without looking at her.

"Jax, can I talk to you please?" She had an idea. If he would hear her out, maybe everyone could have everything they wanted.

"Not now. We're under a time crunch." He still wouldn't meet her gaze.

She wanted to scream.

"This is where I leave you." Lincoln patted Jax on his shoulder. "Watch your back."

"Linc, man, I–"

"Say it and I will punch you square in that pretty face of yours." Lincoln pulled Jax into a man hug, slapped him on the back, and then shoved him away.

"Be careful," Linc said to her. "And take care of him for me."

Heat filled her face. "Jax doesn't need me." Hadn't he made that abundantly clear? Was Lincoln blind and deaf?

"Don't be so sure. Herb, thank you for the hospitality." Lincoln shoved open the door and disappeared into the dawn.

She searched Jax's face for a response to what Lincoln said, but he'd arranged his expression into neutral. Yup, Linc was blind and deaf. Like all men.

"Time to go," Herb said.

They followed him out to the tarmac. A small white plane with red stripes along the side and a high wing span waited for them. Herb helped her climb in, and she took a seat in the second row. She hated flying and had to swallow the lump in her throat that threatened to suffocate her. Four-seater planes were known for crashing, weren't they? Jax climbed in next and took the seat beside her.

Herb found his place in the front and fiddled with buttons and gauges. The dashboard of the plane looked like something straight out of a high-tech movie. He pulled on his headphones and indicated they do the same.

"If you want to hear each other speak, keep these on," Herb said.

She was tempted to take hers off and stay silent for the entire flight. The plane began to taxi, and her heart picked up speed. She squeezed her eyes shut and fisted her hands as they lifted off the ground and the wind cradled the plane.

Jax uncurled her fist and slid his hand into hers. She opened her eyes and met his gaze. The glare that had been in his dark-brown eyes since her no-birth-control confession softened. A thin smile tugged at his lips. Her insides melted. She was so in love with him. How could she have been so stupid to wait so long to tell him? They had lost so much time together and now would never have another chance. She let out a long breath and pulled her hand away.

Jax turned his gaze out the window where he kept it until they landed.

CHAPTER 18

"THIS AIRPORT HAS BEEN HERE since before World War I. It was a training field for the air service." Herb climbed from the plane and gave a hand to Eden to help her down. She tried to ignore the heat rolling off Jax right behind her and failed miserably.

"How far are we from Manhattan?" She jumped down and scanned the area.

They were in the middle of an open field. The runway cut the area in half. Trees stretched out on their right, acres of land to their left was dotted with tiny buildings in the distance, and blue skies up ahead. They were also sitting ducks.

"About an hour," Jax said. He shielded his eyes from the afternoon sun and scanned the area.

"You know this place?" Herb said.

"Well enough. I had a case not too far away once. We used one of the hangars as our home base during the investigation. A car is supposed to be waiting for us."

"Give them a minute. Your driver is my next passenger. Hank worked that out for you too."

On cue, a silver four-door sedan came from the direction of the small buildings. It bumped over the grass and kicked up a cloud of dirt. The car parked feet away, and a tall man with long, brown hair, and a wiry beard to match shoved his way out the door. He grabbed a bag out of the trunk and tipped his cowboy hat at them. His legs bowed at the knees, but his boots were shiny.

"Howdy, I'm Chris." The bearded man shook hands with Jax and Herb. "Ma'am." He removed his hat and nodded at her. "Hank said you could give me a ride back to Chicago."

"Indeed. Whenever you're ready. Nice to meet you both." Herb returned to the plane.

"I filled up that tank for you. Hank wanted you to have plenty of gas to get to Manhattan. When you're done with the car, leave it in this lot. The back row always has open spaces." Chris handed Jax a small piece of paper. "No GPS, but you'll find a few maps of the state in the back seat. Best of luck to you." He tipped his hat again and followed the path Herb took.

"Let's go," Jax said.

She stole one more glance at the plane. All this fuss for her. She could never repay Jax or his boss for what they've done for her. He never even questioned her. She needed him, and he was there.

"Thank you." She slid into the car beside him.

"For what?" He kept his gaze buried in the map.

"For everything. All of this. Your kindness."

"It's my job."

"Maybe I should pay you. I'm sorry I didn't offer it sooner. Whatever your rate is, I'll meet it." It was the least she could do for him.

"I don't want your money. We'll call it even, okay?" He tossed the map in the back and turned the car toward the buildings.

"You mean for the past?"

"Where do you want me to take you? You never gave me the address," he said ignoring her question.

"Central Park West."

"Wow. Is that another King property?"

"My friend Faith lives there. I sent her the tape."

"Can she be trusted?"

"I hope so."

JAX TURNED onto Central Park West as the sun dropped below the tops of the New York skyscrapers. The famous Central Park bordered the roadway on his right. He would have loved a chance to run through there and find that fountain that always showed up in movies but not this trip.

The parole hearing was tomorrow morning. He could drop Eden right in front of the building, drive to Midtown Manhattan and get a hotel room for the night. He wanted to forget about her for a few hours. She had managed to get under his skin and inside his head. He needed to focus on the original reason he wanted to come to New York. Their relationship couldn't factor in at the moment.

"Which building?"

"The one across the street with the tan awning. You can pull over right here." She pointed to an empty spot by the bus sign on their side of the road.

People hurried along the sidewalk on their way to who knew where. A young girl with a black backpack handed money to the hot dog vendor. A large man in black shorts walked his tiny dog. An old man sat on the park bench up against the brick wall bordering the park. He seemed to be muttering to himself because he sat on the bench all alone.

Jax scanned the area. Everything seemed in place. They had made it. Eden could retrieve her tape, expose her uncle, and have her big day. Exactly what she always wanted and he could get back to his life too. So why did his stomach ache so much?

"Thank you, Jax. I couldn't have done this without you." She squeezed his arm.

The heat from her hand sent a current right to his heart. "Sure. No problem. Take care of yourself. Don't trust anyone, okay? Once your story hits, promise me you'll find a place to hide out."

Tears brimmed in her eyes. "I will. You take care too." She leaned in and placed a soft kiss on his cheek.

His heart shattered into a million pieces. He didn't think that was possible, because she'd already broken his heart.

He wanted to tangle his fingers in her hair, pull her against him, and kiss her until she begged him to stop. Instead, he let her slide from the car and cross the street.

He started to pull into traffic. Cars backed up in the

lane coming toward him, blocking some of his view of Eden as she walked under the awning.

She turned her head to look down the street as if someone called her name.

A man with broad shoulders and wearing a baseball cap ran toward her.

Jax's blood started to boil.

She turned in his direction and opened her mouth, but with the windows closed and the sounds of a crowded city all around, he couldn't hear what she said. He slammed on the brakes. A car hit him from behind.

The man grabbed Eden and zig-zagged through the traffic jam toward the park. She struggled against him, but he was too strong for her. Jax jumped from the car and drew his gun.

"Stop. Police." He shouted without thought and aimed at the man in the baseball cap, but he couldn't get a clear shot

"Gun." Someone yelled.

People screamed and ran. Horns honked. The old man on the bench jumped up and stood in Jax's line of vision.

"Move, old man."

But the guy didn't budge. Jax ran after Eden and straight into the park.

CHAPTER 19

THE LONG SHADOWS of day's end crept through the trees of Central Park. Jax kept his gun drawn but pointing up. He followed the lantern lit path deeper into the park. The evening spring air kicked up a cool breeze. Leaves rustled as the wind ran its fingers through them.

Where had Eden and her attacker gone so quickly? Anything could be lurking in the shadows, but he used them to hide his approach and soften his footsteps. Eden didn't call out for him. Either they went a different way or she'd been gagged or rendered unconscious. He had to find her and save her. He would have to stay focused, not get emotional, and end this. He ignored the ache in his leg. The reminder of what happened the last time he lost focus.

A couple holding hands and laughing passed him on the path, but with the night sky cloaking the park, fewer people would be around. He didn't want to call the NYPD for help. Their arrival would tip off the man with Eden, and he would likely kill her. Jax would have to do this alone.

Would they have come this far into the park? Whoever Thomas King had sent after Eden would want that tape. Taking her into the park didn't make a whole lot of sense. She had probably messed up his plans when she yelled on the street for Jax. *Good girl.* But the guy would be panicked, and that meant Eden could get hurt. As long as she was dead, the tape would be hidden. Unless someone else knew about it. But he didn't think so.

He followed the path for what felt like forever but couldn't be more than ten minutes. If they went another way, he was screwed. He'd never be able to find them. "I'm coming, babe. Hang on," he whispered.

And when he saved her, he would beg her to forgive him.

The path ended at the Bethesda Terrace overlook. He eased up to the wall and peered over to the fountain below. His stomach twisted. He took aim, but he was too far away to hit the target. If he had his rifle, this show would be over.

The man shoved Eden's head under the water of the fountain. Jax's vision blurred. He shook his head to clear it. The way down was the wide-open steps. No coverage. No element of surprise. He squatted low and ran across the grass instead and down the slope toward the fountain.

The guy yanked Eden from the water. She coughed and gagged. But the man swung his gaze in Jax's direction. He dropped down flat on the grass.

A pain shot into his left thigh. He bit back a yell and allowed himself a quick look. A rock had cut into his leg where his old wound was. His vision clouded, and sweat popped out on his upper lip.

Eden screamed.

He pushed up, but his leg gave out, and he fell back down. *Fuck.* Gritting his teeth, he shoved off the ground again and leapt over the short wall. He drew his gun and approached.

"Let her go."

"Jax." Eden lunged forward, and the asshole yanked her back.

"Can't do that. I need that tape." The man whipped out a knife and held the tip against Eden's temple.

"Eden, baby, you okay?" He kept his gun pointed at the guy's head and ignored the throbbing in his leg. He prayed he wouldn't have to run or fight, but he would get that knife.

"Shoot him, Jax. My uncle sent him. He's nobody." She struggled against the man's hold.

The knife pricked her skin. A line of blood trickled down her face.

"I need you to stay still, Eden. " At this range, he could hit the guy between the eyes, if he had a clear shot.

This guy's ginger hair poked out from under his cap. His build was solid but not wide. He stood only an inch above Eden, which made shooting him in the face more complicated. There was that and the damn knife.

"You might want to listen to your boyfriend, Miss King. Just give me the tape and everyone goes home." The man sneered.

"Do you take me for an asshole? Because we all know you're the only one not going home tonight." He held his ground, but his emotions churned. One wrong move and Eden could die. "Now, let her go. Tell your boss you missed her. She never showed."

"Sorry. I value my life too much. You won't kill me because you follow the rules. But Mr. King makes his own rules. I'll disappear, and no one will know what happened to me. Or he'll blow up my car with my kids in it. Take me to that tape. We know it's here."

"I'll never give you that tape." Eden elbowed the man in the gut.

The perp bent forward, and the knife cut Eden's face. She screamed, but managed to get her knee up and hit the guy in the throat before falling on her ass.

Jax lunged for her. They could make it to the street, and he'd call for help. He kept his gaze on her face. The blood ran over her chin. She looked the way she did the night she showed up at his house. He couldn't let her get hurt again. He'd never leave her. He'd risk his life to save her and their baby, if there was one.

She reached out her hand. Her fingers were inches away. He tried to grab her, but something collided with his chest, and his feet left the ground. His gun went flying. He landed hard on his back, and the fucking guy was on top of him.

He couldn't breathe. His vision blurred. A fire burned in his leg where the rock cut him, and the asshole's knee pushed against it. A guttural growl started low in his throat and climbed out as he pushed the guy off him.

They rolled on the ground until he could pin the guy between his legs. He wrapped his hands around the man's neck and choked. The guy's face turned red, and he tried to pry Jax's hands off his neck.

The man let go of his hands and shoved his thumb into the hole in Jax's leg. He let out a loud yell and fell back, gripping his leg.

The guy pounced. He punched Jax in the head. The world spun. Eden's face came in and out of focus. He tried to get up. He had to save her, but the spinning in his head kept him down.

The man swung again and connected with Jax's jaw. His head snapped and banged the cobblestone ground.

He covered his head with his arms, but he could still see. The man came at him again. Jax kicked his leg up and made contact, but he didn't know if he did any damage because he had to use his bad leg.

He pushed off the ground and crouched. Where was Eden? The guy came at him like a linebacker. Jax darted to the side, but not before the man collided with him again. He tried to push the man away like he used to on the football field back in high school. The guy stumbled, but grabbed onto Jax's shirt and took him down.

"I didn't want to kill you." The guy kneeled above Jax, pinning him down with his strong legs and one hand on his neck. His throat closed to the size of a straw. The blade of the knife glinted in the lantern light of the terrace inches above his face.

Jax struggled to push the guy off him, but nothing happened. He struggled to breathe. Black spots dotted his visions. He wanted to see Eden before he died, but she was gone. *Good girl. Run. Be safe. I love you.*

He closed his eyes.

~

"GET YOUR FUCKING HANDS OFF HIM." Eden's hands shook as she held the heavy gun against the bastard's head.

She had never held a gun before. She wasn't even sure if she pulled the trigger it would go off. She didn't know where the safety was. But when she saw Jax's gun fly through the air she knew it would be up to her to save them.

She pushed the gun harder against the guy's head. He raised his hands and dropped the knife. She kicked it away.

"Get up. Slowly. Or I will blow your fucking head off." She hoped.

The man eased off Jax. Jax got to his knees, coughing. Blood seeped through his jeans. His bad leg. He must be in a lot of pain. She'd take care of him when all this was over.

"You're making a mistake." The guy held his hands in the air. "Mr. King wants that tape. If you don't give it to me, he'll send someone else."

Not before she got rid of it. She would have enough time to do that and head to Mexico or Wyoming. Or something. "Shut up," she said.

Jax eased up alongside her. "Let me have the gun," he whispered.

She kept it pointed on the asshole but stole a glance at Jax. His lip was swollen and his eye black. He had scrapes on the side of his face. "Are you okay?"

"I'm fine. Give me the gun, babe." He slipped his hands over hers and took hold of the gun.

She was glad to be free of it and wiped her hands on her pants.

"My phone is in my front pocket. If it isn't broken, call nine-one-one and tell them where we are. Then I need you to call Lincoln. Can you do that?" His voice was deep and strong as if he hadn't been wiped across the ground only minutes before.

He was her hero. He always took care of her and protected her. She had been so selfish years ago, but no more. She fished his phone out of his pocket and made the calls.

Jax pointed the gun at the guy until the police arrived.

Jax put his gun on the ground and held his hands up as many police officers ran toward them. "I am in law enforcement."

An officer with a military cut approached them while another handcuffed the shithead that attacked them.

"I'm Officer Coleman." His eyes held the brightness awarded only to the young. A tight smile tugged on his lips.

"I have ID in my wallet. May I pull it out?" Jax kept his hands in the air.

Officer Coleman shook his head. "You can put your hands down. We received a call right after your nine-one-one, and only seconds later, my grandfather called me and told me to get my backside to the park asap even though this isn't my district."

"I don't understand," she said.

"Ma'am, my grandfather is good friends with Hank Patterson. I believe Mr. Patterson employs Ajax Montero. That's you, isn't it, sir? You fit the description, and the situation here fits the scenario my grandfather relayed on my way over."

"I'm Jax."

"You came over because your grandfather told you to? He must be important." She wasn't sure she was following, but did it matter?

"I always listen to my grandfather. Are you two all right? You're bleeding." Officer Coleman pointed to Jax's leg.

"I'll be fine."

"Better to get that checked. I can call you an ambulance. After you get looked at, we'll need your statement."

"It's just a cut."

"Then if you two will follow me. I can take your statement over at the bench. You probably want to sit. I have some water in the cruiser."

"Can we have a minute?" Jax said.

"Sure. Take your time." Officer Coleman sauntered off to the side.

Jax turned to her and cupped her face in his hands. Heat burned her insides.

"You were amazing," he said.

"You were. You weren't even afraid."

He laughed. "Wrong, babe. I was scared for my life and yours. I didn't think I could stay calm enough to keep it together. When that guy had me pinned, I thought it was over."

She wrapped her hands over his wrists. "I can't lose you again. I'm not going to break the story. I'm going to give the tape to Emma. She can expose my uncle, but it won't be because of me."

"People are going to want to know where she got the tape."

"She'll protect her source."

"What are you saying?" He narrowed his eyes.

"I'm saying I never meant to betray your love for me. I love you, Ajax Montero. I don't want my life to go on another second without you in it. Family is what matters most. Not my job. Not some big by-line. Or awards. Those won't keep me warm at night or safe from harm. Only you can do that. If you still want to."

He pressed his lips against hers, and she sighed into his kiss. "Are you sure? You've dreamed about this career."

"Never more. I can still write. Just in a safer way. Especially if I'm pregnant. If you want, I can go with you to the parole hearing tomorrow." She'd stand beside him and help him through whatever he needed.

"I don't need to go." He pulled her against him.

"Why the change of heart?"

"When you were in danger, I knew nothing mattered to me except you. I'm done worrying about the past. Now is what's important. The future. I'm not going to look back anymore. I can write a letter and express why the guy who shot me should stay in jail. I want to move forward. With you. I love you, Eden."

EPILOGUE

NINE MONTHS LATER.

Jax entered his kitchen and smiled. Linc and Serra stood at the counter pouring chips into a bowl and salsa from a jar. The new year promised to bring good things.

"You ready to have your butts beat in a game of poker?" He pulled a beer from the fridge.

"Dream on, buddy." Linc took a seat at the table set with poker chips and a deck of cards.

"Wait for me." Eden brightened the room like the sun coming over the Montana mountains. "It takes me so long to move around. I can't wait to have my body back."

Jax went up behind her and pulled her against him. He rubbed her swollen belly. "You're beautiful."

"I think you've gone blind." She laughed and ran her fingers along his jaw.

Heat ran from her touch straight to his center. If Linc and Serra weren't there, he'd take Eden to bed. He loved her pregnant body. In fact, he couldn't get enough of it.

"You two are cute," Serra said.

Linc narrowed his eyes. "I think they need to get a room."

"You would think that." Serra slapped a kiss on his lips.

"This whole mess started because of a room." Eden waved her hand over her stomach.

"It was a train, babe."

"Can we play before I have to go home and puke?" Lincoln rolled his eyes.

He was one lucky son of a bitch. He took a seat and patted the chair next to him for Eden.

She didn't budge.

"Babe?"

Her mouth fell open. "Game's over."

"What?" he said.

"It's time." She looked down at the floor then back up.

Serra jumped from her seat. "Let's go, men. We're having a baby."

"Now?" Jax stumbled out of the chair and knocked it over.

"Right now." Eden nodded.

"Holy shit," Jax said. He was about to be a father.

"That's one way to put it." Serra grabbed coats.

"Linc, man, will you drive? I don't think I can focus on the road."

"Hell, yes."

Jax scooped her up in his arms.

"I can walk, you know."

"Not tonight."

Tonight they were having a baby.

ABOUT STACEY WILK

Stacey Wilk wrote her first novel in middle school to quiet the characters in her head. It was that or let them out to eat the cannolis and she wasn't sharing her grandfather's Italian pastries.

Many years later her life took an adventurous turn when she gave birth to two different kinds of characters. She often sits in awe of their abilities to make objects fly, make it snow on command, and remain dirty after contact with water. She does share the cannolis with them for fear of having her fingers bit off if she doesn't.

Because of the extraordinary characters in her home instead of in her head, including a king who surfaces after dark and for coffee, she writes novels in multiple genres about family, home, and second chances.

When she's not creating stories in make-believe places, she can be found hanging with the cast members of her house or teaching others how to make make-believe worlds of their own.

Stop by for a visit and make sure to bring some cannolis.
www.staceywilk.com

Or her private Facebook group for her amazing readers –
Stacey's Novel Family https://bit.ly/2FK8Lae

Or her newsletter - https://bit.ly/2A0jEFk

ORIGINAL BROTHERHOOD PROTECTORS
SERIES

BY ELLE JAMES

ABOUT ELLE JAMES

ELLE JAMES also writing as MYLA JACKSON is a *New York Times* and *USA Today* Bestselling author of books including cowboys, intrigues and paranormal adventures that keep her readers on the edges of their seats. With over eighty works in a variety of sub-genres and lengths she has published with Harlequin, Samhain, Ellora's Cave, Kensington, Cleis Press, and Avon. When she's not at her computer, she's traveling, snow skiing, boating, or riding her ATV, dreaming up new stories. Learn more about Elle James at www.ellejames.com

Website | Facebook | Twitter | GoodReads | Newsletter | BookBub | Amazon

Follow Elle!
www.ellejames.com
ellejames@ellejames.com

facebook.com/ellejamesauthor

twitter.com/ElleJamesAuthor

Printed in Great Britain
by Amazon

22140618R00099